Galveston 1900:
A Storm,
A Story of Twin Flames

Ervin Mendlovitz, O.D.

Texas, USA

Galveston: 1900 A Storm, A Story of Twin Flames

All rights reserved. Under International Copyright Law, No part of this publication maybe reproduced, stored, or transmitted by any means-electronic, mechanical, photographic (photocopy), recording, or otherwise- without written permission from the publisher.

Cover art by Allen LaFuente
Edited by: Michael A. Velez II
All photos unless otherwise noted were taken by Aaron Mendlovitz or courtesy of public domain.
Photos edited by In Focus Publishing.

Copyright© 2012 By: Ervin Mendlovitz, O.D.
Printed and bound in United States of America
Second Edition

A special thanks to
Elizabeth and the boys
for their love and support.

Galveston: 1900 A Storm, A Story of Twin Flames

Galveston: 1900 A Storm, A Story of Twin Flames

Blessing of One

" Uniting two halves of one soul is inevitable, but timing depends upon your level of spirituality. When the time is ripe, true soul mates find one another even if they are worlds apart- whether physically, on opposite sides of the globe, or spiritually, with contrasting lifestyles and backgrounds... Here's wishing you the courage to keep growing so that you may know-or continue to know- the Blessing of Oneness."

- Rav Berg.

A special thanks to Rav Berg for his insightful words that served as a source of inspiration to the writing of this book.

Galveston: 1900 A Storm, A Story of Twin Flames

Table of Contents

	Prologue	13
1	Over the Bay Bridge	17
2	Recollections of the Villa	23
3	First Glimpse	31
4	Dinner with Peter, Karina, and the Children	37
5	Clinical Rounds with Dr. Bernstein	45
6	Genevieve's Diary: Hank	51
7	Meeting at the Print Shop	55
8	Genevieve's Diary: First Impressions	61
9	Dr. Isaac Cline	65
10	Pagoda Bathhouse	69
11	Genevieve's Diary: The Heart Locket	75
12	Picnic on the Beach	79
13	Hank	87
14	Genevieve's Diary: The Evening of the Assault	91
15	Recuperating	97
16	At the Print Shop	101
17	Genevieve's Diary: No Way Out	103
18	A Premonition	107
19	Getting Permission	109
20	Genevieve's Diary: The Ring & The Fourth of July	113
21	At the Beach Hotel	115
22	Holidays	119

23	Genevieve's Diary: The Holidays	123
24	The Wedding	127
25	Celebration at the Garten Verein	131
26	Alone At Last	135
27	New Orleans	139
28	Journey Back Home	145
29	An Evening with Friends	147
30	Frozen	149
31	Calm Before The Storm	153
32	Louise Hopkins, Dr. Samuel Young, & Isaac Cline	157
33	Oppressive Heat	163
34	Signs	165
35	The Race to the Orphanage	169
36	The Morning After	177
37	At the Hospital	181
38	Wandering Through the Devastation	187
39	Haunted	193
40	The Butterfly	199
41	Hotel Galvez	203
42	Dinner at The Galvez	205
43	At the Beach	209
	Map Of Galveston	220
	About The Author	223

"Love is sweet captivity." - Czech Proverb

"Only love gives us the taste of eternity." - Jewish Proverb

"The best and most beautiful things in the world cannot be seen or even touched. They must be felt with the heart." - Helen Keller

"What I need has been given to me by the earth. Why I need to live has been given to me by you." - Unknown

Galveston: 1900 A Storm, A Story of Twin Flames

Galveston: 1900 A Storm, A Story of Twin Flames

I have, for an immortal moment in time, tasted Heaven...

And by you, I basked in the soothing glow of Paradise.

- Ervin Mendlovitz

Galveston: 1900 A Storm, A Story of Twin Flames

Breaking Through the Ice

Blinding white engulfed the world, shining mercilessly through every crack and every hole. The only hint of color came from deep inside the ice, a blue tint that spread a cold warning to stay away. Snow piled in drifts around a small lake, as if to hold back the warmth of the sun or keep intruders away. But two young boys - brothers - laughed at each drift and puff of ice. They ignored the warnings, refused to see the storm slowly advancing. There was a break in the clouds - a ragged slice of sun to play in - and they were determined to enjoy it.

Their play gradually pushed them closer and closer to the edge of the shore, until they found themselves hurtling across the ice. Filled with glee, they slung their bundled bodies farther and farther from land, sliding with all the abandon of fearless youth.

"Hey, Uri watch this!"

The oldest boy, Peter, ran a few steps and gracefully slid along the icy surface. Uri laughed and clapped his hands.

"My turn!"

Peter laughed uproariously as Uri pretended to be a penguin by taking little steps and occasionally flapping his arms by his side.

"Peter! Look, I'm a penguin!"

The boys kept roaring with laughter, even as Uri continued his silly little display, moving further out into the middle of the lake. Peter's laughter started to fade, sensing the danger.

"Uri, you're going too far. Come back!"

Consumed by the moment, Uri continued his silliness, unaware of anything other than the pleasure of now. But as he kept moving, tiny fissures began to spread, the unexpected pressure of Uri's dancing feet breaking the ice. Before long, the myriad cracks met and gave way, dropping Uri below the frigid surface. But beneath the frozen water, a current still moved, pushing Uri away and trapping him below more frozen surface. Uri's joy drowned under the weight of his fear as he pummeled the ice with his fists in an attempt to break through. The cold burned him, making his breath fail even faster.

Then a thought filled the expanse of his mind. Was it been a voice? No. It was a mere tendril of thought drifting inside of him, coalescing into the certainty that he was not alone. It was from another part of him, separate yet of him. It willed him to go on, to live.

Now the while, the storm moved closer. Peter leapt into action and dove into the hole where Uri disappeared. Even as Uri banged futilely against the ice, Peter was coming for him, careless of his own life, consumed with trying to save his brother. Knowing there was little time, Peter let the current take him. The light was dim through the ice, the day already darkening. Nevertheless, Peter kept his eyes open, searching for the flailing form of his brother.

Seconds passed, moments that stretched into an eternal now that slowed time down into agonizing flashes of consciousness. The blue edge of the ice. The fiery water, freezing pore after pore. The relentless, unfeeling current. An overwhelming ache inside the lungs. A spot of true black. A slash of white and red. Fingers, outstretched, desperate. A numb touch of hands. Then time resumed its pause, almost rushing in its hurry to return to measurable certitude. Peter grabbed one of Uri's fists and pulled against the current. Uri latched on to Peter, who freed his hand and devoted all of his being into pushing his way back, back, back.

With a Herculean effort, muscles straining, air nearly spent, Peter dragged Uri back to the open hole in the ice. With a final surge, Peter and Uri broke the surface, wheezing in great gasps of air – precious air that seemed bent on pushing them back under the water. Peter, knowing his strength was waning, quickly heaved Uri onto the surface. Uri lay there on his back, choking, desiring nothing more than to fall into sleep. But he heard his brother, still in the water, and forced himself to turn over onto his knees. He crawled to the edge where Peter was tiredly trying to pull himself out of the water. Uri again latched on to one of Peter's arms – this time to begin pulling. Peter strained and threw his leg over the icy lip. With a sudden pop, Peter surged completely out of the water and fell half on top of Uri.

Neither one moved, their bodies stunned by their efforts, their minds numbed by the implacable confrontation with Death, which had previously been nothing but a shadowy fable they scared each other with at night. Then the storm arrived. Wind gusted and blew, infiltrating their soaking clothes and burrowing inside their blue-tinged bodies. They once again heaved themselves upward, this time to their feet. With Peter in the lead and Uri firmly attached, they struggled to the shore, shaking and weak. Once there, the work really began as they tried to fight their way through the snow. But it was too much. Uri's strength quickly gave out, and he fell. Peter stopped and picked him up, but before long, Peter, too, fell to his knees, unable to move. They huddled, half-frozen, believing it was their end.

Uri looked up, away from the false warmth of his brother, into the face of the storm. It was fierce and strong, dark and threatening, thick with clouds, armed with ice and wind. But it was also beautiful and wild. Uri decided that if he was to die, he wanted his last sight to be the storm, in all its magnificent fury. He closed his eyes and slept.

Light. Heat. Voices. Painful remembrance as his body relearned to feel. His father patting him awake. Uri opened his eyes. His father's worried face peered above him, the storm whitening his beard as he leaned over

"Uri."

"Da? Peter!" His father smiled in relief and hugged him close.

"Spasibo Bozhe (Thank you, God.") He heard his father whisper.

Uri heard voices and realized he was being moved.

"Peter is okay. You're okay. We're taking you home."

Uri's eyes darted around, and he finally understood that his father and a few neighbors had rescued him and Peter. He wasn't going to die. He had escaped the storm. But his eyes wandered back up to the sky. Mortality lived in him now. Call it fate or the will of the Universe, but he knew, deep down, that the storm had begun to define his life. And Uri also knew... it was only the first storm.

Galveston: 1900 A Storm, A Story of Twin Flames
CHAPTER 1

Over the Bay Bridge

Texas Heroes Monument

The ride was interminable. We were headed east and in the distance I could see amongst the trees, the small town of Texas City before we passed over the bridge. Droplets poured in mournful streams down the windows, blurring the view of the coastal country. The flat ground soaked up the water, pools forming where the ground was already saturated. I could hear the car's wheels swishing through the fluid, that essential component which without, life could not exist... A liquid that, at the same time, like a double-edged sword, so duplicitously, in an instant, could turn as a Giver of Life to the Slayer of the Living. An earthly manifestation of the Tree of Good And Evil.

I looked up at the gloomy dark sky, searching for a break in the clouds. But they stretched on, unending, as I so vividly remembered. The distance refused to melt away, despite the speed of the rented Chrysler limousine.

A true Texas storm. The wind picked up and whistled around the vehicle, its sound blending into remembered wails that pieced through that night. My eyes flicked back to the road and through the downpour, I was able to make out the slender span of the bridge to Galveston Island, a long causeway flanked on either side by two train trestles. My driver, Alan, stared intently ahead, the flash of the wiper blades showing brief slices of the road in front of us, clarity following blurs, back and forth. Other than the swish of rain, it was quiet, still, and hushed inside the limo. Were we in a cathedral? Or part of a funeral procession? Alan's voice broke the silence.

"Some weather."

The droplets distracted me again, reflecting long-lost faces.

"What?"

"I was referring to the weather, sir." It took me a moment to respond, grief unexpectedly closing my throat.

"Oh, yes… It certainly is."

The bridge began to take on distinguishable features. The dark spaces became recessed arches through which the ocean flowed, the span a straight, flat expanse stretching across the Bay, dim lights spaced at intervals.

Alan once again broke the silence.

"Dr. Petrokov, I apologize as I forgot to give you this telegram back in Houston. It's from Dr. Flemming."

Alan pulled the letter out of his breast pocket and reached back to hand it to me. I took it slowly, knowing that no matter what it said, it would always be too late for me.

"Thank you Alan." I opened the letter slowly, already rejecting any comfort it might try to offer.

April 2, 1945.

Dear Uri, I must again thank you for your assistance with the Penicillin research. I owe a great deal of my success to you. Now, before you become too conceited old chap, I want to remind you that most of the success has been as a result of my perspiration alone. Recently, however, I have really enjoyed the good life, and I feel you played a role in my leisure. I certainly wished that you had been there to celebrate the Nobel Prize with me.
Your friend and colleague, Alexander.

As the car we crossed the bridge, my mind briefly drifted back to my challenging work with Dr. Fleming. I'd achieved my Ph. D. in Biochemistry, driven to help discover a way to cure infection of the body. After long years of work, there had finally been a breakthrough. Modern medicine had reached a new peak. Millions of lives would be saved. Not that it mattered. Dr. Fleming's thanks could only ever ring hollow. I shook myself out of my dark thoughts and looked out across the Bay. The sight that greeted my eyes was another ghost of my past. Instead of a steady patter, I saw sheets lashing the sea, the Bay battered by gigantic waves amidst the furious pounding of the wind and bullet-like rain. The Hurricane filled my vision; I forcibly blinked the memory away.

"Do you mind if I turn on the radio, Sir?" Alan asked.

"Go ahead."

Turning on the radio, it crackled to life. Alan soon found a station.

"...liberated by the American troops a monstrous atrocity has been uncovered. The Camp was liberated by the 4th Armored and the 89th Infantry Divisions. The Ohrdruf Concentration Camp is located in the very heart of central Germany and apparently was a killing factory for Jews and Gypsies. This is George Clough reporting on KLUF Galveston."

After a brief pause, the same voice on the radio continued.

"Well folks, there you have it, the rumors of German atrocities that have persisted throughout the War seem to be true. I will be opening the phone lines and invite our listeners to share their thoughts on this new development and whether or not too little was reported on stories leaking out of Germany regarding genocide and ethnic cleansing."

The killing and casualties of the War were mind-boggling. I had heard of the rumors of the German plans to create an Aryan "master race" and was repulsed and sickened to hear how ethnic and religious prejudice had reared its ugly head again. So much death, so much hatred. My heart was pained with sympathy for I had personally seen and experienced both. Having crossed the bridge, I directed Alan to travel east along Broadway. The palm-lined esplanade was so much wider than the narrow shell-paved street through which horse drawn trolleys served as convenient sources of transportation many years before. I saw the *Texas Heroes Monument* with its stately female figure standing at its pinnacle, proudly unsheathing her sword. I remember the joyous celebration as the Monument was dedicated on the anniversary of the Battle of San Jacinto, the conflict that gave Texas its Independence from Mexico. The long parade and festive band music celebrating the Statue's unveiling occurring a mere six months before the tempest struck.

    The engraved word, "Honor," flashed at me below her granite perch. Honor? I didn't believe there was any in my return. As the car drifted along in the rain, we passed soaked gas stations and crying residences along the street. Yes, I could have gone another way, a shorter, less painful route lacking all those wrenching reminders, but I didn't. Instead, I shuddered as each street scene flashed scenes of the past, specters glaring accusingly from every corner. Yet how could they blame me? I was broken yet living, a man who had once been whole. Still, slivers of that time pierced at me from the corners of my eyes. I wanted to remember bliss, but as I glanced side to side down alleys and through storefronts, all I could see was devastation. A world destroyed. My world ended.

    So why not take a short tour of the Island that I used to treasure so much, that had been my first real home after leaving Russia as a young man? I stared out of the window almost hungrily, letting the familiar ache spread through me. It was time to return home.

    "Turn left up ahead at 10th Street."

    Alan made a left and passed my old haunt, the Medical School at Galveston. The massive, red granite three-story baroque structure was the same building that existed when I lived there. It had survived the disaster. The wind gusted, parting the rain for just a moment, and I saw a flash of the Medical School, drowning and battered from many years before, windows blown out under vast arched recesses. I sighed, letting the ghostly memory fade of its own accord. Considering my return to such an emotional part of my past, it was useless to fight the visions my mind conjured.

    "Left at Strand Street at the next intersection."

    Alan followed my directions smoothly and executed the turn without mishap. We drove slowly along The Strand. The street that had been - and was still - the central business district. Still, there was little traffic. Many of the stores were boarded up, ruined by yet another colossal calamity - The Great Depression.

But in my mind's eye, I saw the glory of what it used to be – a marvelous collection of architecture that so impressed me when I first arrived in America. Despite the grime and neglect, I could still see a downtown that had not, unfortunately, escaped the perils of time and circumstance, but whose faded and ravaged beauty could still be glimpsed.

As we continued driving west, we passed storefront after storefront, each one with tenants quite different from the ones I remembered. The once teeming streets were now sparsely filled with pedestrians; some who appeared quite impoverished mingling with working people and servicemen from the *Army Air Corps*. Where were the consulates, the fine furniture stores, and the clothes stores that sold the height of turn-of-the-century fashion, the pedestrians dressed in their Sunday best? Where were the tantalizing smells of bakeries and exquisite restaurants that filled the street with the aroma of French Cuisine, sizzling steaks, and fresh Gulf seafood? Instead, I was confronted with a cheap souvenir store, a near empty diner, a grimy barbershop, and the square façade of JC Penney's.

Time had erased so much of what had always been my heart's home. And I wasn't sure, on seeing all the changes time had wrought, whether or not I was glad only echoes remained. After all, time had marched on, but in many respects, for me, the hands of the clock had stopped that day. In all the years since, I had felt half-submerged by memories of crucial moments that I could have changed. Should have changed. There was nothing truly new and precious for me left to experience. Instead, I'd indulged my self-pity and relived my memories thousands of times. Actions and precious seconds that would have meant the difference between true happiness and agony.

So as we reached the midpoint of The Strand at the north end of 21st street, it hit me like a blow to the gut, stealing my breath as I looked at it still standing there… the abandoned and boarded front of what was once our business, *The Galveston Printing Company*. Gone. There was no denying the reality of it standing forlorn and dilapidated in front of me. No denying what was past. Now it was nothing more than an empty, forgotten ghost of a building. I sighed as yet another flash overlay my sight, and instead of the shining memory of the Strand's heyday, this time I saw heavily damaged and even completely demolished buildings. There were enormous mountains of debris everywhere - bricks, wooden blocks, roof parts, clothes, shredded trees and forgotten, mud-trampled toys.

Alan's voice again nudged me away from the violent images in my mind.

"It certainly is not what it used to be."

Another flash of piled corpses erupted behind my eyes.

"A lot of things are not what they used to be."

Taking off my glasses, I wiped them with my handkerchief and quickly dabbed the moisture of my eyes as we approached our next turn.

"Alan, another left at 24th."

He made the turn smoothly and we continued our drive to the *Villa*. The rain subsided, but the day still remained drizzly and gray. At last, we rolled to a stop at my destination - a beautiful three-story residence with red brick and ornate iron trimming from the turn of the century. The garden was immaculate and splendid, full of colored flowers and many green plants. Numerous large trees shaded the grounds. A matching turn of the century iron fence guarded the house.

As we rolled to a stop, I couldn't help staring with bittersweet longing. It hadn't changed much after all, the beautiful villa in which I once lived, nearly a lifetime ago. A deep ache squeezed my heart and I nodded to myself almost absently. It was time. I stepped out of the limo before Alan could open the door.

"Alan, get five white roses and thirteen red ones. I will be here till you return."

Alan nodded quickly and looked at me expectantly.

"Anything else sir?" I smiled, unable to voice my true wishes.

"No, that will be all."

He jumped back in the limousine with the grace of youth, and I sighed, thinking again of happier times.

As Alan drove off to complete my request, I was left alone standing in front of the house, a light drizzle falling around me. I slowly walked toward the gate, peering through the bars at the *Villa* I had once so loved. The life I once loved. This time, as my vision blurred, I let my memory take over my mind. One that had been severely thrashed by the full fury of the storm replaced the quiet *Villa*. I breathed in deeply, letting the horrible memories come cascading back, moisture filling my eyes. Then I went back even further, beyond the destruction, to the day it all began. Yes, it was time.

Galveston: 1900 A Storm, A Story of Twin Flames
CHAPTER 2

Recollections of the Villa

Uri's Villa

It was 1898. I was 22 years old, full of optimism and the zeal to live life fully and completely. My brother's wife once called my demeanor radiant, especially when I was in the process of learning something new. But all I thought was how much opportunity there was for me in America, especially in regards to science. As for my older brother, Peter, he was the rock on which I stood while trying to figure out how to thrive in such a different land. Yes, Peter and I had excelled well beyond any expectations, but yet in many ways we remained unchanged.

Our material comforts had not changed our hearts and attitudes to those around us. Conversely, it amused me to see that money did somewhat diminish the disdain that the established aristocracy had toward us. Even so, despite all that we had managed to accomplish, there was always a nagging awareness of something missing, something not of the world of success, money. Something calling me, a missing piece.

Nonetheless, I felt very grateful and blessed for my life as it was. After all, I knew that perfection existed nowhere. But I liked to pretend I was content, for I was young and yearned for new adventures. Thus it was that I left our print shop with a glad heart, looking forward to the next chapter in my life, on which I believed I was about to embark.

Our shop was located on The Strand at 21 Street, and I crossed the main street through downtown. I was in a horse-drawn buggy on my way to meet my brother at a house I was interested in purchasing. I looked over to the docks and though I was moving along the high point of the Island - a mere 8.7 ft. above sea level – it was still a rather flat perspective. The ships sailing to and from the docks appeared to be floating parallel to the thoroughfare I was moving along. I laughed aloud at the thought of ships floating down the street. Before long, the buggy soon pulled up to an Italian villa at Broadway and 24th with a "FOR SALE" sign in front by the ornate, delicate-looking, black wrought-iron gate.

Peter was already waiting in front, no doubt expecting me to show up late. But I glanced down at my watch-piece and saw I was just on time. My brother's solemn face turned into a grin as I stopped the horse and hopped off. At thirty-one, he looked quite the successful businessman in his dapper suit. With a Bowler perched on his head, he was fairly tall and had an erudite quality about him. In the six years since he opened the print shop, he experienced a good amount of prosperity, which he shared with me. I thought myself very lucky to have him for an older brother. His voice rang out with a noticeable Russian accent, much like mine.

"Hello, Uri. Horosho u sdelali eto vovremja. (Nice of you to make it on time today.)"

We both chuckled. I turned and looked at scenery in front of me. The residence was absolutely breathtaking - a grand three story red brick residence adorned with a matching black wrought-iron porch that also extended to the second floor. The spacious grounds were perfectly manicured with plants, palm trees and some large oaks.

"What do you think, Peter?" He turned his gaze back to the Villa.

"Se vohdnya krahsevah (It is beautiful.)"

We waited there, staring at the magnificent mansion, while my realtor, Mr. Hackett, came and opened the gate.

"Good afternoon gentlemen. How are you today? Lovely day isn't it?" he said with a slight Texas accent. I nodded effusively.

"It certainly is!" I gestured to Peter.

"This is my brother, Peter Petrakov." Peter and Mr. Hackett exchanged a handshake as Mr. Hackett introduced himself.

"Mr. James Hackett here to serve you."

"It's a pleasure to meet you." Mr. Hackett beamed at Peter.

"The pleasure is mine. Now, if y'all would please follow me."

We all walked back towards the house. Mr. Hackett proceeded to show Peter and me into the house's receiving area. It was a large, impressive room already filled with Victorian furnishings. Along the back wall was a magnificent set of stained glass windows that provided a backdrop to the carved stairway. Mr. Hackett turned to my brother.

"As I have told Uri, the furnishings come with the house. The owners have relocated to New York City and did not want to transport anything there. As you can see, this house is among the finest Galveston has to offer. As you can see the interior has been outfitted with Renaissance style. We have here fifteen-foot high ceilings, five bedrooms, and three baths. It also boasts a library, music room and ten different chimneys. It even has a solarium. Let me show you the dining room."

I stared around, entranced, smiling with approval at everything. The curtains on the wall. The wood curio by the teak sideboard. The high ceilings arching overhead. The warm light of the afternoon sun shining through the windows. It was obvious from my demeanor that I was truly enchanted with the house. Peter clapped me on my back and chuckled again.

Mr. Hackett turned into a side room.

"And here is the dining room. Quite lovely." He noted raising an eyebrow.

Peter nodded in agreement as he strolled in behind Mr. Hackett. I brought up the rear. I stopped at the threshold, caught by the idea that it was all so close to being mine. That house, that room. And what a room it was. Fine art decorated the walls, while lovely drapes adorned the windows. There was an elegant collection of Victorian furnishings – chairs, sideboards, and a large, ornate mahogany dining table that dominated the center of the room. But it was the beautiful gas chandelier that caught my attention, hanging from the center of the ceiling, sparkling merrily. I could picture holidays, parties, and celebrations. Mr. Hackett didn't linger, however, so with good cheer we moved through the back doorway to the Butler's Pantry.

"The Butler's Pantry… It acts as a buffer between the odors coming from the kitchen and the dining room. Very cunning design I should say." Mr. Hackett added.

He showed us the glass cabinet where the china was stored. Next to this was the sink with both hot and cold running water. On the opposite wall was the pantry for baked goods. We now ventured from this room and into the kitchen. It was spacious and typical of the era.

Mr. Hackett pointed out the latest amenities.

"Here we have a gas-burning stove – a vast improvement over coal if you ask me. There's also a large sink with counter on both sides and as you can see, plenty of pantry space for the groceries."

I smiled again at Mr. Hackett, who was so clearly pleased to be showing the house. He then gestured to an oak icebox lined with enameled metal that was located in the adjacent hallway that led to the porch outside.

"This set up provides easy and convenient access for the iceman and milkman

"Mr. Hackett, this kitchen is truly a marvel!" Peter clapped me on the back.

Peter's wife later told me when she saw it that any woman would love it, hinting at my bachelorhood.

Peter, though, was much more direct. He absently rubbed his waxed mustache.

"He won't be spending much time in here!" Peter quipped.

I just shrugged my shoulders slightly.

"Why don't we look at the bathroom next?" Mr. Hackett suggested.

We turned and followed Mr. Hackett out of the kitchen down the hall. Mr. Hackett gestured us in with a flourish of his hand.

"It is complete with running water, which is a far cry from most Galveston residences."

Peter turned and gave me a sideways smile, and I winked at him in return. I knew what he was thinking. Running water. We weren't commoners any more. Grabbing the top handle of a large, rectangular wooden piece of furniture, Mr. Hackett pulled down a hideaway bathtub. He looked at it with satisfaction.

"The latest from Montgomery Wards. It costs over $100." He stated, obviously trying to impress us.

Mr. Hackett politely gestured us onwards.

"The master bedroom is upstairs, third floor. If you would please follow me."

We trooped up the stairs and made our way to what I hoped would soon become my bedroom. It was exquisite, filled with more Victorian furniture - a magnificent canopy bed surrounded by mosquito net, a set of matched wardrobes, a wood desk with matching chair, and a small settee. Art also decorated the walls, as I saw a few works by Claude Monet and Charles Gleyre. Along the wall facing the bed was an exquisite, carved granite fireplace.

I looked out the north-facing window. The wharf was twelve or so blocks in front of it, which allowed a cool spring breeze to bring in the smell of fresh cotton from the *Gulf City Cotton Press Company* that occupied three city blocks between 29th and 31st Streets. The massive warehouses turned bales of loosely picked cotton into compact bales that were loaded onto trains and ships for transport to textiles in New England and Europe. This earthy scent mingled with the mint smell of pine harvested from the forests of East Texas and processed at *The Hildenbrand Planting Mill*. A faint aroma of coffee percolating from the Roasters at Mechanic and Market also seemed to waft through the opening. I turned my head and looked through the view at the eastern window.

"Peter, look!"

Peter turned his head and walked over to that window.

"Very nice view. I think I see the roofs of the *First Baptist Church*, *Ball High School*, and the Synagogue. Isn't this just lovely?" He remarked.

I turned back and looked over the room.

"That it is."

After that, Mr. Hackett led us out to the back lawn, where a multicolored garden was blooming, flowers and vines and trees were budding. After standing quietly for a few moments and taking in the view and the soft sounds of birds chirping, Mr. Hackett addressed us again.

"I'm sure there's plenty to discuss. I'll leave you two here and get the paperwork ready in the dining room." He stated this time raising both eyebrows. I could see how eager he was to close the sale.

I turned away from the scenery, anxious to hear Peter's thoughts.

"Well, what do you think?"

"It's a fabulous home. The only thing that will be missing is a wife and children."

I grinned back, betraying the pang of hurt I felt inside. No, this part of my life in Galveston had not been so easy. Many of the ladies did not appreciate foreigners, especially those with funny accents.

"But not forever I like to think."

"No, little Uri, not forever, especially if you are thinking to buy this house."

I nodded in agreement.

"Yes, Peter, I am."

"What is the asking price?"

"150,000 dollarov."

"Ne vsyo to zoloto chto blest it." (Not every glittering thing is gold.) It is a magnificent residence, but I'm sure I can negotiate the price down."

I remained silent, my enthusiasm somewhat deflated.

"Very well, how can I deny such… enthusiasm? It will all be fine. Let's go talk to Mr. Hackett."

We leisurely strolled back inside and made our way back to the dining room, pausing to look at a painting or statuette gracing the furniture and walls. Mr. Hackett was sitting and ready for us when we walked into the dining room. The mahogany table seemed to swallow him up, but I was caught again by the sparkle of the chandelier.

It was Peter who turned to Mr. Hackett to begin negotiations.

"How much is the asking price?"

"One hundred and fifty thousand dollars."

Peter nodded at the figure.

"I know my brother is very eager to buy, but first we must discuss this price. That's where I come in."

Peter sat down next to Mr. Hackett and pulled the paperwork closer. I sat down a few chairs away, letting him work without interruption from me. He was an extraordinarily wonderful brother, and as I looked around that elegant, spacious room, I already knew it would be mine.

A couple of hours later, we were on the buggy and headed back to town. Keys jangled in my hand, the weight reassuringly pressing into my palm.

"Quite the negotiator. You saved me a lot of money."

Peter beamed back at me.

"It is called the art of closing the deal. You may be the passion behind the business, but I'm certainly the brain.... Not the first time I have saved your behind."

Rueful laughter spilled out of me.

"I can't argue with that."

We proceeded to go downtown while I contemplated my new home. Home. Such a strange word in a way, a strange idea to think of it that way, there on that small Island full of heat, humidity, and salt – so different from the house in which I grew up in cold, frigid Russia. What a life, I thought, that I could have such a beautiful home. My own beautiful home. What pride I took in my abilities. But there was something else calling, coming closer every moment. I could feel it.

Galveston: 1900 A Storm, A Story of Twin Flames

Galveston: 1900 A Storm, A Story of Twin Flames

CHAPTER 3

First Glimpse

The Strand

A couple of weeks later, it happened. Though it took me a bit longer to understand why, no matter how I filled my days, I had never really felt truly fulfilled before. The day was rainy, and I decided to enjoy a walk from our print shop to a restaurant further down on the Strand where I would have lunch. The downtown streets were paved with flash hammered wooden blocks and the walled curbs are knee high, so it was easy enough to stay out of the muddy street. As I strolled through the Strand, I heard the unmistakable sound of a steamship chugging into port at the Wharf just a couple of blocks north. As the cloud of smoke from its funnels drifted overhead, I heard a voice hail me.

"Uri! What fine weather we're having!" a familiar voice rang out.

Smiling, I turned to face Isaac Cline, a thin middle height man in his late thirties with a wide mustache. He was commenting about my walk through the rain. Of course, as he was the resident meteorologist in charge of the Weather Bureau Station located on the Island, he had every right to tease me in such a manner. I waited for him to catch up, then continued onward, matching my quick step to his rather more leisurely ones.

"Good morning. Mr. Cline."

"Morning, Uri." He said looking at me with his animated eyes.

I looked up and gestured to the ominous clouds filling the sky.

"When is this supposed to clear?"

"Well, I'm on my way to the office to get the telegraph report from Washington."

Mr. Cline's office was located on the third floor of the *Levy Building*, three blocks south of the Strand on 24th street. I sidestepped a large puddle before responding.

"Still centralized forecasting from the Capital?"

Mr. Cline shook his head in admitted disapproval.

"Silly system we have. My personal forecast is usually more accurate than those DC bureaucrats. From yesterday's barometer readings, we should be sunny in two days."

"Ah, very good then. Thank you."

Mr. Cline nodded and tipped his Bowler hat to me, then headed across the street toward his office. *The Levy Building* was a plain amber bricked building surrounded by a multitude of tall, narrow rectangular windows, with a sign from the third floor that proudly proclaimed *"National Weather Bureau Station, Galveston, Texas."*

A clap of thunder sounded overhead, followed by a gust of wind that carried off Isaac's hat. My gaze followed the path of the hat when a buggy caught my eye. Only it wasn't just my vision that was captured.

Before I fully focused on what I saw in the distance, I felt something emanate from deep inside my being. It interrupted my breath and froze me for a few moments. As I made out two ladies in the buggy, the feeling only increased. The first woman who was holding the reins stared sternly ahead, her face creased in a frown. She appeared to be middle-aged. But it was the second that quickly stole all my attention and made my breath return and heart beat ever more quickly. She was young, not yet twenty, and stunningly beautiful. Her face was a mixture of intelligence and thoughtfulness.

Captivated by this stunning young woman, I came to a standstill and watched the carriage turn a corner and ride out of sight. A singular sense of déjà vu came to me, and for some reason my mind turned back to those terrifying moments when I was under the ice. The abrupt sensation inside me gradually faded, and in its absence, I finally identified it: for a few moments, I'd felt truly connected and.... whole, as though my entire life journey had led me to this singular moment. Filled with this idea, I pensively made my way into Peter's and my business, *"The Galveston Printing Company."* It was located across the street from *"Ritter's Café and Saloon,"* and the smells of fresh bread and frying meat followed me inside as I opened the door to the shop. I was immediately met by the scents of paper and ink, and the twin smells of food and work mingled overhead as they usually did while I stood on the threshold and took in the view.

The Print Shop was an extremely successful business established by my brother six years prior. It was alive with activity as our seven print operators rushed in and out filling orders. Peter and I, on the other hand, worked as supervisors and took orders from the customers. I turned my head towards Peter's bookkeeping desk where it stood behind the order counter. There was a wall partition behind the desk that separated the front area from the ten large printing presses.

These machines were state if the art for the time, manufactured by *Miehle Printing Press & Manufacturing Co.*; with the large three wheeled side and two metal plates through which the paper was fed. They enabled us to print invitations, business cards, stationary, and even hard bound books, a commodity in those days. My eyes drifted back to the front of the shop, which had been allocated to counters that displayed samples of the types of work available at the shop. I made my way over to my desk, which was situated a few feet from Peter's. My brother, meanwhile, was busily working through financials and budgeting for the coming week.

Peter looked up briefly when I came in, his eyes already glazed with the purposefulness of his work.

"Is the order for the Mexican Consulate ready?" he said with the business tone I came to expect.

I consulted an order sheet on my desk.

"Most of it is complete. It will be ready tomorrow."

"Very good."

He wrote a quick note on a ledger and continued working. Before I could tease him, the door chimed and I turned to see who it was. It was Dr. Young, who was both an amateur meteorologist and Secretary of the Galveston Cotton Exchange. He was a tall lanky man about 50 years old with a long slender nose and prominent forehead. He'd been in the shop several times, and I eagerly turned to the sales counter as he walked up to it.

"Dr. Young… Good afternoon. How are you?"

Dr. Young nodded cordially at me. His slit eyes twinkling slightly.

"Very well, thank you." I pulled out an order form.

"More stationary?" I said anticipating his request.

He nodded almost sheepishly, as if he couldn't quite figure out how he was going through the paper so quickly.

"Yes, we are running low."

"You would like the one with *'Galveston Cotton Exchange'* written across the top?"

"That's it. I need two thousand copies."

I nodded and pulled out an order form. As I filled it, I made some idle conversation, as I was known to do in my youth.

"How's the cotton crop this year?

Dr. Young gave me a large smile.

"A record, my boy… a record. How's the family?"

I glanced across the room where Peter was busy working.

"Just as grouchy as ever."

Peter turned with a half smile and rolled his eyes at me. I grinned back, and grabbed a separate book for receipts.

"Your order should be ready by Friday."

I put the form in a basket labeled "ORDERS," the name Dr. Samuel L. Young printed neatly on it, before handing him another slip of paper.

"Here is your receipt, Dr. Young. We certainly appreciate your business!"

"Thank you, Uri."

As Dr. Young walked out of the shop, I saw Peter from the corner of my eye. He was reaching for a fountain pen, but as he began to write, he realized that I had played yet another prank on him by removing the tip.

Peter snorted to himself.

"That brother!"

I went back to work with a mischievous smile, already mentally planning the next trick I might play. The long day passed in a flurry of work, but I enjoyed myself immensely. All the while I could not stop replaying the beautiful vision of the young lady riding in the buggy.

I never had felt so good, so productive, so animated. After our employees had left for the day, I pushed back my chair and began to lock up the windows and equipment. When I finished, I went back and leaned over my desk to enter a few final notes in a logbook. Peter, meanwhile, was counting a large stack of money.

"We've been busy." I said. Peter nodded in agreement.

"Indeed. If this keeps up, we will need to expand." He said as he rubbed his mustache.

I finished the last entry with a flourish and closed the book. Straightening my back, I spread out my arms as if to embrace the shop.

"What a country! The land of milk and honey, or as they like to say here "the happy hunting ground."

Peter finished counting the money and locked it away.

"Yes… so many opportunities here. So much to do, so many people to meet."

He looked at me intently with that sly smile of his.

"What are you getting at?"

Peter leaned back in his chair.

"Did you like Mr.Hadley's daughter?"

I shrugged and put my elbows on the counter, my brow wrinkling in thought.

"She seems to be a nice young lady… but no chemistry."

Peter laughed heartily at that.

"Always the scientist."

I cocked my head at Peter.

"The ladies of Galveston are not that fond of Russian men."

Peter's smile faded a little.

"They're not fond of any foreigners" and then he added *"Eto escho tsvetochki, a yagodki vperedi (These are just flowers; berries will come soon)."*

I could always count on him to try to keep my spirits up. I nodded. It was a land of milk and honey, but though a War had been fought decades before, there were still plenty of prejudice still alive, dividing people for senseless reasons.

I sighed. The moment, however, passed quickly as my natural optimism reasserted itself.

"I want to invite you and the family to dine at my house… a celebration of my new residence."

I'd show him how much use my new kitchen would get.

"We would enjoy that."

"Sunday?"

"Yes. That should be fine."

Peter stood up and we gathered our frock coats. It was time to go home.

As he locked the front door and we began walking down the street, an image of the girl from the morning rose back in my mind's eye. I stared at the spot where I had last seen her, turning away out of sight. For me, that spot somehow now had a new meaning. I could feel that it had a different vibration to it. A tight core of wonder was curling inside me, still dormant, but ready to push the embers of my soul into unfolding its sheared edges.

For it was meant to be a flame.

Certainty then set in: I would see her again. The Universe had willed it to be so, at this time at this place. Nothing could stop it. And there would be no more waiting. No more edges.

Just unity.

Galveston: 1900 A Storm, A Story of Twin Flames

CHAPTER 4

Dinner with Peter, Karina, and the Children

The Grand Opera

I spent many nights working late, and then falling asleep still dressed at my desk. Mama's refrain, *"Kuy zhelezo, poka goryacho." (Do things while it's the best time to do them.)*, definitely had been ingrained in me. But it wasn't print work that occupied my mind. Instead, it was the fascinating studies on Chemistry and Biology that stole hours from my sleep. I would read them into the early morning hours, the scientist in me elated at the many discoveries being made. But there was just so much to learn. I felt as if I was racing time, trying catch up before I could really contribute to the science world.

One such morning, I was awakened by several loud knocks. I managed to rouse myself enough to see that it was after sunrise. The roosters hadn't managed to wake me, nor the magnificent golden rays that streamed past my curtains. I was still dressed in my clothes from the previous day, and I was stiff from slumping over my book-covered desk. I had been particularly engrossed in *"The Complete Chemistry"* by Elroy Avery, and in fact had actually fallen asleep upon its open pages. What completely fascinated me about Chemistry was how the scientist was now able to take chemicals and combine them in such a way, usually employing a thermal process, to create something new! It was like tapping into Divine power, creating something novel that never existed before. It was as though the lore of Alchemy, a legend that has been with mankind for thousands of years, could one day come true. These incredible thoughts raced through my mind as I had been reading Mr. Avery's book. Several more knocks sounded out, and I roused myself enough to respond.

"Yes, come in."

The door opened to admit Mary, a pleasant, lady I'd hired to look after the house. She shook her head at me and started straightening the room.

"Just your wake up call, sir."

"Yes. Thank you Mary." I muttered groggily.

There was just so much to do, so despite my exhaustion, I scrambled to my feet, straightened my suspenders and headed out of the door. Just as I reached it, I turned back to face Mary.

"Tonight, the family is coming over."

She gave me a quick smile and kept working.

"Of course, sir. Don't worry yourself. I've got everything prepared for tonight."

"Mary, you are a wonder."

She shook her head as she gathered a pile of clothes that I had left at the side of the bed.

"Off with you now. Didn't you tell me how much work you have to do today?"

She was right, of course. My dinner would be well earned. Later that evening, we sat down to a fabulous dinner – Peter, Karina, their three children, and myself.

"Mary, you've outdone yourself!" I announced.

She beamed at me as she straightened her white skullcap and white apron. She then proceeded to arrange dishes on the table. Peter was looking under dish covers with Sergei, his seven-year old son, while the girls, Sasha and Annie, were giggling at each other.

"Ah! What is this, little Sergei? Black caviar? And this? Potatoes and mushrooms, good. What about… this one? Beef stroganoff! Did you know this is Uri's favorite dish?" Peter asked playfully.

I pointed my fork at Peter while addressing Sergei.

"Did you know your father's favorite is *shashlik*?"

"Is that lamb?" Sergei responded, his brown eyes widening.

Peter chuckled.

"Yes it is, Sergei."

Sasha then spoke up.

"Uncle Uri, my favorite is oladi."

"Well I don't mind if we sample a little dessert beforehand."

I reached out and speared one of the little pancakes slathered with sour cream, then proceeded to stuff the entire thing in my mouth. Everyone started laughing.

"Uri, you're spoiling the children! They're going to start demanding dessert now." Karina's voice was teasing, so I knew my sister-in-law wasn't truly upset with me.

I shrugged and grinned, then lifted a glass of vodka and waited for the others follow suit.

"A toast to this joyous occasion." Everyone rose his or her glasses.

"Toast!" added Peter.

"Toast, Uncle Uri!" Sergei blared out.

We all took a sip, the children grimacing even though their vodka was watered down.

"Peter, please lead us in prayer." Requested Karina.

But before Peter could commence, Karina noticed Sergei slouching at the table.

"Sergei, please sit up straight."

"Yes, mama." Sergei replied with a touch of embarrassment.

I winked at him just as Peter began.

"Let us bow our heads. Dear Lord, we thank you for this special occasion and this lovely house that my brother bought. Please fill it with health, love and prosperity. Thank you for the bounty that you have placed before us. Amen."

We all chorused, "Amen" and began to eat. Mary hovered, checking to make sure everything was fine with the food or if we had any last minute request. Karina took a dainty bite before starting the dinner conversation.

"I saw Cora Cline at the grocery store today. She said that she and Isaac attended the premiere of *"Macbeth"* last Saturday at the Opera - an absolutely delightful play she said. Peter, we should go."

"Sounds like a splendid idea, Karina. I'll buy the tickets this week."

She smiled at him and the love echoing in the air between them made me ache with envy. Karina then took another bite of food.

"The meal is absolutely exquisite." Peter nodded vigorously and spoke around a mouthful of *shashlik*.

"Indeed." My own mouth full of stroganoff, I waved at Mary, who flashed one of her small, reserved smiles.

"We can all thank Mary for that." I finally managed to get out.

Mary gave everyone a quick look before turning to me.

"Will there be anything else, sir?"

I shook my head and pointed to the food with my fork.

"That will be all. Thank you. Now go eat."

Mary left the room to go have her dinner in the kitchen, though I had told her there was no need to be so formal. But she wouldn't hear of it. The sound of forks and chewing filled the air for the next several minutes. Just as I was convinced I might finally be filling up, little Sasha's voice finally piped up.

"Father, could we go to the beach tomorrow?"

Peter lifted his eyebrow at me as if to indicate that I was to blame for the question. I merely shrugged my shoulders. Could I help it if I admired the beach?

"First you and Sergei must finish your homework."

Sasha did not seem too pleased with that prospect as her face wrinkled in dismay. I could see her trying to think a way around it. She looked up at her mother, then Peter, and then me. I nodded at her and she finally sighed.

"Do we have a deal, Sasha?" Peter asked with a touch of firmness in his voice.

She replied rather glumly as she looked down.

"Yes, sir."

Karina frowned at Sasha's tone even as Peter smiled. As I looked to Sergei and Annie, who were both busy eating *oladi*, I felt a familiar emptiness echo inside, pushing against the satisfaction of having my family eat Sunday dinner inside my very own home for the first time.

After dinner was concluded, the children were sent into another room to play though I daresay I didn't have quite the collection of toys that were available at my brother's home. Still, this gave us adults the chance to talk away from the children. We were sitting in the large parlor. As Peter savored a cigar and I my pipe, I pulled out a letter I'd recently received from our Mother in St. Petersburg, Russia.

"I have a letter I wish to share with you."

Peter looked up and met my gaze. He grunted in acknowledgement. There was only one person whose letters I'd share. He leaned forward as I took a breath and began reading.

> "Petia podelelsia so mnoy radostnoy novostew. Rasskazal kakoy krasivey dom y teba, I starause predstavit sebs. Ne mogia seve predstavit chto ve tak rasbogateete e tak krasivo aschevete za 8 korokich let. Shin pre zare dovoino tyashelaya no mne pomogaet misi shto mow senovia pyinyaly pravinow reshinie novue shizn v Americe. C Bolshoy lubovie za vas. —Mama."

The Russian felt comforting in my head, even as my eyes automatically translated the letter:

> Dear Uri, Peter has told me about the wonderful news. I imagine your house to be quite beautiful. I never dreamed how successful you and Peter would become in just 8 short years. Life under the Czar has been so difficult, but it is eased by knowing that my sons made the right choice by starting a new life in America. With much love and pride, -Mother.

I realized we'd been sitting there silently for several moments, absorbing the words. The touching letter had spoken to each of us.

Peter spoke up.

"Hopefully, one day soon we will be united again."

"Amen," I added, knowing that it would be quite difficult for her to leave. Or for us to return anytime soon.

We all stood there in silence, unwilling to admit what we were all thinking. After a few minutes, though, Peter noticed the books on my reading table, ***Nature's Wonderland*** and ***The Principles & Practice***

of Medicine by William Osler, the father of modern Medicine.
"Still studying?"
My fingers trailed over one of the covers of the book as I contemplated my answer. How could I explain the need inside me to learn all that I could about the sciences that could impact the body? That could heal the sick and save the dying? But I kept my answer short.
"Every chance I get."
Karina looked at me in astonishment.
"Have you read all those books?"
"From cover to cover, Karina. We certainly have discovered much over the last 30 years."
Peter placed his hand on Karina's back and rubbed it gently.
"He's been interested in this a long time. In grade school, he always had his own "science experiments." Of course, most of the time, his "analysis" involved Mother's cooking ingredients."
There was a hint of pleasured teasing in his voice. My face flushed with embarrassment as I recalled the many experiments I thought I'd successfully conducted, only to end with a scolding from my mother.
"Yes, well, Mother wasn't too pleased."
Peter laughed at the rueful expression on my face. Then his look turned serious as he considered the books scattered everywhere.
"Uri, why don't you spend some time at the Medical College? I heard that the Chemistry Department is looking for some volunteers."
Karina smiled at me.
"It sounds like a great opportunity, Uri."
Surprise colored my response
"But what about the shop?"
Peter spread his arms out as if to embrace the entire room.
"We'll just have to do without you some of the time."
Realization dawned on me – my brother had been planning this for some time. Elation quickly followed and I turned to Karina, playfully apologetic.
"He'll be lost without me. You'll have to deal with more of his temper."
Peter looked at me pretending to be offended and quipped.
"Lost?... *Yaytsa kuritsu ne uchat. (Eggs don't teach a hen.)*"
Karina laughed and I joined in, followed only after a moment's pause by Peter. Filled with gratitude, I rushed over to my brother, pulled him away from Karina, and enveloped him in a hug, pounding his back as hard as I could. Truly, I had the best brother any one could ever hope for. Now, it was time to turn some of those elusive dreams I had into reality.

Time to become the scientist I always wanted to be. Time to figure out the next chapter of my life.

Galveston: 1900 A Storm, A Story of Twin Flames

Galveston: 1900 A Storm, A Story of Twin Flames

CHAPTER 5

Clinical Rounds with Dr. Bernstein

Old Red

A few weeks later, I found myself working as a researcher in the *Galveston Medical College* where I had quickly made friends with several other young scientists, including another laboratory researcher named Michael Williamson. Michael was a pleasant young man from the east coast who had studied at the *University of Pennsylvania* in Philadelphia. When he heard that Texas had established its first *Medical College* at Galveston, he headed west to become the head of the *Research Department*.

One April day found us both working together in the *Research Laboratory*. The room, located on the third floor at the far end on the corridor, had fast become one of my favorite places on the island, filled as it was with chemicals, flasks, and other apparatus on many shelves that lined the walls of the room. It was suffused with a palpable creative energy and was the first place that I truly felt that I could finally, possibly start to make a real difference in the world. It was wonderful and empowering to know that we were conducting experiments that could one day be duplicated by the First Year Medical Students during their required Chemical Laboratory Course. Research that could improve the health and well being of humanity.

Michael and I were busy tallying the results of a recent experiment. As I stirred a final solution into a beaker, Michael peered into his microscope. After a few minutes of stirring, a white precipitate appeared in my beaker. Michael now stood up, made a few marks on the papers next to him, and then began to stretch. Then he looked over at me, observing the contents of the beaker.

"Uri, once you have finished, you may want to join Professor Bernstein. He will be conducting his daily rounds." He said with his unmistakable New England accent. I blinked up at him in confusion.

"Rounds?"

"The professor will be reviewing the status of numerous patients who have been placed under his care. Third Year Medical students follow him during these rounds. Dr. Bernstein encourages the volunteers to join him as an orientation to the hospital. Justus seemed to have enjoyed the experience quite nicely. Are you interested?"

It just took me a few seconds to respond.

"Certainly."

Justus Schott was the other volunteer, a druggist who owned a Shop close to City Hall. His skills in Chemistry were quite accomplished.

"Good. I'll make arrangements."

Accordingly, a few days later, I found myself back at the *Galveston Medical College* – only this time I was in the medical wing, which was full of patients. There were four medical students waiting as Dr. Bernstein and I joined them. Dr. Bernstein was a distinguished man in his fifties, suffused with an air of confident authority. We were congregated in the main hallway that led to the rooms where the patients were convalescing. The hallway was busy with others milling about, passing us by in both directions. Dr. Bernstein introduced me to other young men.

"Gentlemen, this is Mr. Uri Petrakov, a new volunteer. I want Uri to see the human side of research as well as how specimens are collected before they are sent to the laboratory."

Dr. Bernstein began discussing the first case as we walked down the hallway.

"Our first patient today is a 58-year-old male who suffers from a heart dysfunction."

It was a fascinating turn for me, for I had never really seen the actual connection between the work I did in the lab and the way it was used to help people. But it was the last patient of the day that made the most impression on me. Her name was Sarah Ferguson. The four students and I now stood together outside of the door of her room as Dr. Bernstein explained her malady.

"The final patient is a 32 year old female who has developed pneumonia. I checked her temperature earlier and it is quite elevated, indicating a severe infection. Her breathing is becoming quite labored."

One of the other students spoke up quietly, though I daresay we all already knew.

"What is her prognosis?"

Dr. Bernstein looked at all of us quite soberly.

"Terminal. The inevitable will come. At this point we can only be supportive and make her as comfortable as possible."

Dr. Bernstein then gestured us into the room.

I immediately caught sight of Mrs. Ferguson, who was lying unconscious, her face flushed and her breathing overwrought. Her forehead was covered with a wet wash towel that had been soaked in a bowl of ice water– an obvious attempt to bring her body temperature down. A man was seated by the bed – presumably her husband, for his face as he raised it was distraught and tear-streaked. His glance took all of us in as he greeted us quietly and simply, mingled hope and fear in his voice.

"Hello doctors." He barely croaked.

"Hello." Dr. Bernstein replied softly.

Mr. Ferguson returned to staring at his wife as Dr. Bernstein began a close examination of the patient. We stood silently as the doctor listened to Mrs. Ferguson's lungs and then heart with the aid of a stethoscope. He then inserted a thermometer into her mouth waited a few minutes. I saw his countenance sink as he noted the reading. Dr. Bernstein finally leaned back, and addressed Mr. Ferguson with a solemn sigh.

"Have you noticed any changes?"

Mr. Ferguson looked away from his wife to answer Dr. Bernstein. He spoke quite softly, his voice ragged with pain.

"She has stopped responding to the treatments."

Dr. Bernstein nodded his head once sharply as if confirming what he already knew.

"The disease is progressing rapidly."

"Doctor, is there anything you can do for her?" asked Mr. Ferguson

"I'm afraid we can't."

Mr. Ferguson became teary eyed, and I looked away, not wanting to intrude on this very private moment. Still, I saw out of the corner of my eye as Dr. Bernstein put his hand on Mr. Ferguson's shoulder and spoke with gentle compassion.

"We are truly sorry for you. We will keep her as comfortable as possible."

Sorrow lay heavy over all of us students as we left poor Mrs. Ferguson lying in her room, her bereaved husband hopelessly holding her hand. When we were several doors down the hallway, Dr. Bernstein turned to address us.

"Tomorrow I want you to follow up with the patients we have seen today. This evening review the first 5 Chapters of Campbell's ***Flushing & Morbid Blushing: Their Pathology and Treatment***." We will meet again tomorrow for a brief conference after Obstetrics."

The other students turned and walked away, but I stayed with Dr. Bernstein. The pain and suffering I'd seen weighed on me heavily, and I felt as helpless as the dying patient we'd just left.

"Dr. Bernstein, it was certainly was difficult to see all this... Mrs. Ferguson in the prime of her life."

Dr. Bernstein regarded me steadily for a moment, then exhaled solemnly, looked away, and took off his glasses. He slowly stroked his neatly trimmed gray beard, and he spoke with an honest, acute awareness of someone who knows the limits of his powers.

"We need medicines to kill the bacterium that cause infection and disease. Ever since Joseph Lister introduced the concept of sterile surgery, medicine has come a long way to understanding the process of microbial disease and infection. In fact, one of the required courses that First Year Students attend is Hygiene. Unfortunately, in terms of killing these invisible invaders, medicine remains far behind the challenges that man has already conquered."

I nodded silently in agreement.

"Just look around: steamships crisscross the oceans, telegraphs provide almost instant communication from one part of the country to the other, and lights illuminate the night. Yet when it comes to curing patients, once a microbial infection has set in… we are still in the Dark Ages."

As an after thought he added, chuckling slightly

"Believe it or not, I still know some doctors, old timers, who still believe that the best cure for infection is bleeding the patient."

"Talk about the Middle Ages." I quipped back.

In truth, I'd never considered that side of scientific advancement before – knowing just enough to realize that we could do more to cure the sick, but being not yet capable of doing so.

"That is why the work that you and Michael do is so vitally important." He said emphatically. The doctor continued walking with me following.

"It will take laboratory research to give Doctors the tools to combat the illnesses that plague humanity. That's why I encourage you people to make rounds with me to show you where your efforts are headed."

"We have so much to do. Thank you, Dr. Bernstein. For all of this – even the tragedy."

At the main hallway we parted ways, and I climbed the stairs back to the Research Laboratory.

CHAPTER 6

Genevieve's Diary: Hank

14th March 1899

Oh! That wretched man just doesn't understand! Why can't Mother see that he is no good for me? I was just leaving The Galveston Hat and Shoe Co. where I had just purchased a lovely straw hat this evening, ready to return home. But just as I stepped out, I saw Hank standing at the bottom of the stairs – waiting for me. (Mother thinks he is quite attractive, but I disagree. Perhaps it is not so much looks, but that he lacks the bright energy of ambition, the innate sense of what to do and where to go, or even what he wants from life. Other than me... Besides, I'm sure he gets blotto from time to time, as I could swear that I have smelled beer on his breath on more than one occasion.)

When Hank saw me, he presented me with the biggest smile and a little bow. I'm sure he thought was elegant but I thought was rather awkward. I know I should try and be polite to everyone, but I admit that I didn't even bother pretending to smile back. All that had ever done was encourage him, and now he just follows me around. I tried to keep our conversation short, but I'm not sure he understood.

"Hello, Genevieve – " he said in that awful Texas drawl.

I gave him a curt "Hello." But he persisted.

"How have you been?" He looked so silly with his hat in hand.

"Fine." Of course here was when my temper started to get the better of me again. How dare he stalk me?

"What are you doing here?"

"It was slow at the railroad station so they let me off early. Would you like me to walk you home?" Thinking of Mother's joy at seeing us walking together made it quite easy for me to refuse.

"No thank you." I thought that might be it, and made as if to walk past him, but he stopped me by reaching out his hand and placed it on my elbow! The nerve! And then:

"Would you like to go to the dance at the Garten Verein on Saturday?" I gave him a haughty refusal, but he still didn't understand.

"Well, we can do something else – " And my temper finally started to show itself.

"No, Hank. Not Saturday night, or afternoon, or any other time! Now I really must be going."

Then I turned and walked away, leaving him behind me. I hurried to a busier street heading toward Bath where I could catch the Trolley home, grateful for the press of people that assured Hank wouldn't follow and make a scene. As I was walking, an elderly lady in front of me tripped on one of the wooden slats that line the road and spilled her groceries everywhere. Of course I immediately ran to help the lady.

"Are you all right?"

"I think so my dear." But just as I helped her load her groceries back into her bag, I saw Hank coming up the street after all – even though I thought he was headed in the opposite direction. Fortunately, the kind lady afforded me a reasonable excuse not to linger.

"Which way are you headed?"

"Home. Three blocks south of here."

"Perfect. I'll walk you."

We then turned and proceeded away from that busy street, I glanced back, expecting to see Hank staring after me. But instead, I saw him disappear into a saloon!

As if that is a proper way to start the evening. Of course, it is likely that he is a regular but just as we were about to turn the corner there. I can only imagine how a conversation would go"

"Hello, Hank. You're here early today."

"Yeah, I got off early."

"The usual?"

"That will suit me fine, Bert." *The pleasant bartender then retrieves a bottle of beer and gives it to Hank, who eagerly drinks it. Yes, it's quite clear in my head. Hank, drinking beer after beer, and me, telling Mother clearly that Hank is nothing but a wastrel. But somehow I think she'll find a way not hear me. She is quite accomplished at that.*

I know there is something more waiting for me. I felt it at once when Father had first mentioned his transfer from Houston.

The island is magnificent. Even my three mile buggy trek to the Orphanage is a joy. Just the other day on the way to the Orphanage the sounds of birds chirping filled the air. I saw families of spoonbills and brown pelicans feeding in the marshes. Overhead above the trees were seagulls that seemed to escort my journey.

I feel as if I was always destined to be here. I just don't know when or where I'll find what is waiting for me. And of course, I am new to Galveston, but it is not a terribly large island, and I do so wish to meet more people. Mother of course says that I shouldn't be so distant, but then she always is insisting that I spend time with Hank instead of letting me decide whom I should spend my time with.

I can't wait for Father to come back. Then I will have a good excuse not to see Hank and have someone who sides with my decisions.

Galveston: 1900 A Storm, A Story of Twin Flames

CHAPTER 7

Meeting at the Print Shop

Galveston Daily News

Less than a week later, the most consequential, final shift in my life took place. For some reason, the days leading to this one were particularly extraordinary. Everything from the research at the College to the business activity at the Shop ran with ease and effortlessness. It started as a typical day at the Shop. Peter was busy in the back checking on the printing presses, while I was recording entries in the business log. The door jangled as more customers walked in, but I didn't look up, as I was just finishing up with the last receipt. The sound of shoes clacking over the wooden floor approached. I finished notating and looked up and into the face of a rather attractive, but nonetheless, dissatisfied-looking woman.

"Good afternoon ma'am. How can I help you?"

The woman's lip immediately curled into a sneer at the sound of my voice.

"Russian?"

She was one of those who apparently didn't appreciate the influx of immigrants. Though I couldn't see what difference it made that I was Russian, if our print shop was offering a reasonably priced and high quality product. Still, she was a potential customer, and I knew I had to treat her with the utmost respect.

"Yes, madam" – She interrupted me, waving her hand at the counter.

"I would like to get a price on some invitations."

I sighed inwardly while straining to maintain my bland smile. Things had been going so well that I could not let this crabby woman dampen my mood.

"First we will have to choose a style…"

My voice trailed off as I was literally drawn to noticing another woman lingering at the front of the store. Something about her seemed familiar, as if by looking at her posture and the curve of her shoulders, I was reminded of someone I knew... Someone I always knew.

She turned in what seemed to be slow motion and looked up; meeting my gaze for what seemed to be an indeterminable number of seconds, for time seemed to stand still. My God, I realized that she was the young lady I had seen riding in the carriage a number of weeks before. All the air rushed out of my body, and I felt frozen as something inside me, an essence of my energy, rushed outward and into her lovely eyes. At the same time, I felt some essential part of her swirl and connect within me. I felt my heart lighten, as it seemed to beat higher in my chest. I knew her… I had always known her because she was the other part of the fire, the other part of my very essence. For the first time in my life I had felt absolute and total connection. Russian mystical lore had called it a "twin flame."

I had neither totally believed nor understood the concept until now. For the first time in my life I was beginning to feel whole. A voice shook me back to the present as the other woman intruded.

"Sir? Can I get some service here?"

It was the older lady, her voice filled with impatience. I nodded at her automatically and turned to address her, though I couldn't keep my eyes from occasionally glancing at the other woman, almost afraid and unwilling to lose any sight of her.

"I'm sorry. Let me get my book which has all the sample invitations."

Quickly, I retreated to the back to fetch the sample book. When I returned, I handed it to the woman, an idea germinating in my head.

"Here it is. Take your time. If you will excuse me, I will go pull some sample invitations from the front. I'll be right back."

Without waiting for a reply, I turned and headed to the front of the shop where the girl stood looking at the sample invitations that were on display. These were the same ones that I had supposedly come to take.

"May I help you Miss?"

Perhaps I'd just imagined what I'd felt. Maybe there really was no circuitry in the air between us before. But as she turned to face me, I once again felt the absolute rightness and certainty of being in her presence. I felt that everything in my life before had led me to this very moment. Our very beings seemed to vibrate at the same frequency. Our eyes met, and words died inside me as I lost myself in her sharp, intelligent gaze. After a moment of staring at each other, a blush crept up her face and she shook her head.

"I'm just looking." Her voice was rich and melodic, and I strove to appear unaffected.

"I… I have more samples I could show you if you don't like these."

She smiled at me, and my gut clenched at the incredible beauty of her face.

"I know. My Mother is looking at them."

Her mother? That lady? It was then I realized that that was the lady who I had seen driving the buggy.

"Oh. I didn't realize that you were together."

She flashed me a look that said she understood exactly what I was thinking about her Mother. As our gazes sharpened, the look changed into one of admiration. I knew she was looking at me with as much intensity as I was looking at her. It was true chemistry in its purest, prime form, and if anything, I understood what to do with that.

"I'd like to introduce myself. I am Uri Petrakov."

With a short bow, I held out my hand to her. She brought her hand up and extended it towards me.

"I'm Genevieve –"

Before Genevieve's hand could meet mine, her mother rudely interrupted, pulling at Genevieve's arm and tugging her away from me as if I was something disgustingly mangy... and foreign.

"Come along Genevieve. The service here is awful. Let's go."

Genevieve's mother sniffed in my general direction and, escorting Genevieve by the arm, marched her out of the shop.

A stunned silence descended as I was left there with my hand still outstretched. The air that had been so alive and charged between us immediately died. Slowly, I dropped my hand and watched the two women walk across the street and recede out of sight. After they both disappeared out of view, I returned to the counter, my expression troubled. Peter was standing there looking at my ledger, but he quickly noticed my dismay.

"What happened?"

How could I possibly explain?

"An incredible *denushka* just came in."

A small smile appeared on his face.

"This has you troubled, little brother? A beautiful girl in the shop?"

I shook my head helplessly, trying to express how I felt.

"She was... like no one I've ever seen before. She was... perfect... But, uh, her mother was not so fond of me."

At this admission, Peter laughed out loud and clapped me on the back. Surprisingly, I felt much better. After all, if Peter believed an angry mother was no problem, why should I?

"Well, I got her name." Silence once again enveloped me as the sound of her name whispered out of me for the first time.

"Genevieve."

"So?" My brother prompted me. I gave him a look of mingled determination and happiness.

"I will find her."

We both returned to our work, but the entire time, I kept seeing Genevieve's face in my vision – her sparkling eyes, her perfect smile, her graceful neck, her strong hands. I was keenly aware of the part of me, deep down inside that ached to the point of pain to see her again. And I would find her. Nothing could stop that; because now I knew she existed. There was no other choice but to locate her again. It was inevitable, a destiny that could not be stopped. I would find her because… she was the other half of my very being.

CHAPTER 8

Genevieve's Diary: First Impressions

2nd May 1899

Today the most incredible meeting occurred! Mother is, of course, quite cross with me. She sent me up to my room where I am supposed to be reading. Currently, I am in the middle of H.G. Wells "The Time Machine" and although I tried continuing the novel, all I could think was of him. I even tried to skim through a couple of other books, but I could not concentrate. Finally, I thumbed through Freud's "Studies in Hysteria" with some vain hope to better understand Mother - all to no avail. I must first write of – him!

The previous few days have been particularly delightful, even Mother had been unusually pleasant. The city is vibrant with spring and the blooming of oleander and jasmine. Well of course Mother wanted to find out about printing some invitations for a party she is planning, and she heard about this wonderful print shop on the Strand. When I went in, I didn't really pay attention to anyone in the shop, for I knew Mother was about to abuse some hapless worker there. But something finally pulled me around, and I looked straight into his eyes.

It was as if a window to my soul opened. I felt dizzy as blood rushed to my head. He almost glowed, and something inside me rushed towards him, magnetism on a spiritual level, something I could not have ever imagined before.

Dear sweet Uri... so handsome, so sincere, and so... familiar. Of course he came to meet me, speaking with a lovely European accent. He managed to extricate himself from Mother and made his way over to see me.

I was pretending to be quite interested in the invitations in front of me, but I was really trying to compose myself, stealing glances toward him as not to appear too forward or rude. Truthfully, I didn't want to take my eyes away from him.

FINISH

Oh! The most wonderful news!

I just looked out of the window to see a horse approaching. Who else would come here this time of night except Father! And sure enough, as the horse pulled up and a figure dismounted, I saw that it was Father, finally home. I rushed downstairs and out the door to greet him before anyone else even knew he was there. I gave him the biggest hug, and his familiar smell enveloped me as his arms came around me. I had missed him so much. But now he is back, so perhaps Mother will stop being so impossible. And perhaps I can somehow arrange some way to return to the Strand… and the print shop… and Uri. Dear sweet Uri! Yes. Somehow I know I will see him again. I have absolutely no doubt that we will meet again.

CHAPTER 9

Dr. Isaac Cline

The *Medical College* occasionally held lectures with guest speakers, and I'd made it a habit to attend all of them if at all possible. These lectures gave me the opportunity to expand my knowledge outside the confines of the College and Galveston itself, and out into the wider scientific community. Thus it was that, along with many medical students and other interested parties, I attended a lecture by Galveston's resident meteorologist, Dr. Cline. Although I'd spoke to him on a regular basis, I had not spent much time pondering or discussing meteorology, and thought I might enjoy his presentation.

Dr. Cline stood behind a podium in one of the College's moderately sized lecture halls. He was speaking of the connection between health and weather – something I'd never considered before.

"So you see gentlemen, my training in *Medical College* and weather has enabled me to see links between the two. Another example: before storms many elderly patients report an ache in the joints such as the knee. I believe that this is related to a drop in barometric pressure. For years, Doctors have reported interesting medical phenomenon that accompany hurricanes. Cyclones have been suspected in triggering premature labor and the bursting of aneurysms. Again, probably related to drastic decreases in barometric pressure."

What an astounding claim! And yet I knew that he must be on to something, especially as I'd always felt strangely connected to great storms in the sky. Unfortunately, that was the end of his lecture.

"Before we adjourn, are there any more questions?"

A young Medical Student raised his hand – someone I hadn't seen before.

"A number of years ago you wrote an article in the **"Galveston News"** stating that any fear that Galveston would be damaged by a severe hurricane is an absurd delusion...Would you please explain?"

Dr. Cline looked somewhat discomforted by the question, but he answered it easily enough, although I must say with a slight tone of arrogance.

"We know that the course of a hurricane follows a parabola. The point where storms curve northeast always occurs between the Bahamas and Cuba. Thus, Galveston would avoid a direct hit. In addition, the Island is shielded from storm surges by the topography of the region. Thus my concluding, that Galveston has no need to worry regarding the threat of cyclonic activity."

As I listened to Dr. Cline's explanation, my scientific mind rose up in protest. It didn't make sense to me that any storm, especially one as powerful as a hurricane, could be simplified down to a few rules.

Nature defied man's effort to tame it – it always had. Great civilizations have been upended by Nature's unpredictability. But then Dr. Cline brought up another aspect that I hadn't considered.

"Gentlemen, you must remember that we are in a race with Houston to become the major port of the West, a race that we are winning. This talk about Galveston being obliterated by a hurricane is a propaganda campaign by our competitors in Houston." He related, the disdain heavy in his voice.

The skepticism in my face was echoed by several others sitting around me. Commerce. Capital gain. That's what Dr. Cline's stance was about. Forget scientific accuracy. He was simply supporting a different type of propaganda – one meant to undermine the competition rather than attract support and more research from the scientists on the island.

"Thank you, gentlemen." He concluded with a tone of self-satisfaction on a job well done.

The audience gave a nice round of applause and I found myself joining in automatically so as not to offend Dr. Cline. Besides realizing the hidden agenda behind Dr. Cline's position, this evening I had seen another aspect to Dr. Cline that I had not known before. It hit me with the words he wrote- "absurd delusion." Bravado was a trait that I found fairly common to the residents of the Island: an optimistic overconfidence that bordered on arrogance. This sureness perhaps stemmed from the importance of the City to the colonization of Texas: Galveston was the first major port in Texas. The Island with its naturally deep harbor fostered a convenient settlement point for the colonization of the New World.

The settlement of Galveston mirrored that of the great cities of the northeast such as New York and Boston where ship friendly harbors led to stops from which European settlers disembarked and built great cities that then served as springboards to the interior lands. Galveston was the Nation's largest cotton port as well as the fourth largest port city, with more than thirty ship lines dropping anchor at its docks. As an entry point for immigrants, it was considered the Ellis Island of the West. As for business, Galveston was likewise referred to as the Wall Street of the West with at least thirty stock companies.

As the essential Texas City, it boasted many firsts. Included in its list of Texas firsts was that it was the first to have electric lights, telephone service, an opera, an insurance company, a post office, a naval base, a cotton press, and a hospital. It blustered three concert halls, over twenty hotels, more than five newspapers, more than fifteen consulates, and 500 saloons- more than New Orleans. Galveston ranked third in the

Nation in the number of millionaires per square mile. Many residents were keenly aware and proud of all these facts. They knew that lived in a vitally important city distinguished with commerce, art, and culture.

    I must admit that my viewpoint differed from that of many of my fellow residents, perhaps stemming from the fact I was born on foreign soil. Although I had considered myself to be an optimistic person, I did not share in this confident swagger. My thoughts in a whirl, I left the lecture hall. As I mounted my buggy and headed toward my home, dusk was setting in. Ahead in the street before me, were a multitude of fireflies playfully igniting the darkening, evening sky. My mind drifted back to the lecture with a nagging and uneasy feeling... pondering and wondering if we scientists had doomed Galveston to a premature demise from our sheer indifference to the truest power in the world – Mother Nature. And I had cause to remember: when the storm comes, there's only so much fighting a man can do before he either escapes… or succumbs.

Galveston: 1900 A Storm, A Story of Twin Flames

CHAPTER 10

Pagoda Bathhouse

The Pagoda Bathhouse

Courtesy of The Rosenberg Library, Galveston, Texas

Rosenberg's Women's Home

The day after Dr. Cline's somewhat unsettling lecture, I was riding in my buggy, on my way to meet Peter for some business for the Shop. I arose early that day before dawn as the contentment in my heart seemed to free me from the usual amount of sleep that I was accustomed to. I decided to ride down along Bath Ave toward the Gulf. Periodically, I would take this route so that I could see the ocean before going to work. It was a way of clearing my thoughts and had a calming effect on my being. I rode the buggy following the rails of the trolley line. Overhead was the electric wire which powered the car. I remember how when I first arrived to Galveston, the trolley had been pulled by horses and shortly thereafter was converted to electricity. I now passed through the residential area of the city where the plants and trees were in full bloom. The oleander and sweet smell of jasmine mixed with the light scent of fresh, morning salt air. I heard the intermittent crow of roosters as they welcomed the light of morning. An occasional gust rustled the palm leaves from the palm trees that could be found throughout the neighborhood. Everything seemed so alive and animated.

I passed *Rosenburg's Woman's Home* with its perched cupola pointing up into the Texas dawn as if saying, "the sky is the limit." Everything seemed filled with such potential. Nearing the shore I could now clearly hear the gentle melody of the waves as they moved to and fro. From here the trolley veered left and continued out on a trestle over the Gulf, traveling by Midway, the business district along the beach, before connecting to downtown along Broadway Ave. Riding just ahead, I saw the *Beach Hotel*, the magnificent Victorian resort that was a favorite amongst the tourists who visited the Island. Just past this I saw the boardwalk which led to a pier that connected to the *Pagoda Bath Company*, a structure that housed showers and changing rooms for those going to the beach. *Pagoda* ran parallel to the beach and extended over the water. It even had a Cafe and restaurant where one could dine while viewing the panoramic expanse of the Gulf.

Though my business was urgent, the walkway to the Bathhouse pulled me closer. As I approached hither, my gaze was drawn to a solitary figure gracefully walking along the pier. A broad smile covered my face, and I hurried to find a spot to tie my horse. I then rushed down the boardwalk and onto the pier, slowing my steps only so as not to startle her. By that time, Genevieve was midway down the pier. She stopped just before the downward set of steps that led to the water below.

It was an exquisite morning, made even more striking by the sight of Genevieve staring out at the alluring blue waves of the ocean. I took her entirely into my mind- tall and slender, her soft cream-colored, draped dress, her mass of flowing hair, and her superb posture. As I approached her, her stance changed, stiffening in anticipation – she somehow knew I was close. Slowly, she turned around to face me. I stopped only a foot away from her.

"Genevieve..."

I called out, her name flowing so easily from my lips. Her eyes lined with extensive lashes met mine, widening as a stunning smile spread across her red lips.

"Hello… Uri."

When she answered, something familiar in her voice harkened me, for a brief instant, to what I had heard when I was trapped under the ice.

A few moments passed as we gazed at each other's face and then into each other's eyes. The familiarity of knowing one another required that no words be exchanged. I calmly... drowned into the large, dark pupils of her eyes. Fully and totally absorbed in the moment, I communed with my other half. I had discovered the portion of my being that had for so long lain dormant. It was a part that I always knew, even if my awareness had been only at some vague, subconscious level. I had become an uninterrupted version of my authentic self and wondered how I could ever have endured as I had before.

"I really wanted to talk to you back at the shop, but your mother was not pleased."

Through smooth, silky skin that radiated with a healthy glow from having spent some time outdoors, I could see her blush prettily.

"I'm sorry...Mother is…. Mother…" She said with regret, slowly rolling her eyes.

She turned away from me, slightly embarrassed by her Mother's behavior and looked out over the ocean again. The rising sun bathing her face in golden brilliance as she reminisced to a more pleasant thought.

"I love seeing the Gulf from here. It makes me feel so calm. My parents..."

"Would bring you here when you were little."

She turned to look at me in surprise.

"Wow… How did you know?"

"I just did."

She cocked her head at me becomingly.

"Such a lovely accent. Are you from Russia?"

"Yes."

For a brief second, I wondered if, like her mother, if that would matter, but Genevieve only smiled at me even more warmly.

"How very interesting."

I couldn't help laughing at her description.

"Interesting? No, it's freezing there. One time it was so cold that my eyelashes fell out."

Answering laughter came from her.

"You're joking."

I nodded my head, acknowledging the joke.

We both fell silent, but it was a silence rich with promise and suspense. She stared out across the waves, but all I could see was she. Her face lifted in a smile and she turned to face me, stealing my breath. Such beauty she had. I would have gladly spent all day staring at her, but responsibilities tugged me away.

"I am on my way to meet my brother. We have an urgent business matter that I can't miss, but I must see you again."

She turned towards me fully, her body scant inches away from me. I could smell the scent of her lovely skin as we shared the very air between us. Her breath was honey sweet.

"Yes… I will meet you here."

"Tomorrow?"

She cocked her head, thinking.

"Six O'clock?"

I smiled down at her and nodded in agreement. Neither one of us moved as I slowly reached up to cup her cheek.

"Until then, Genevieve."

She said nothing, just leaned into my hand and smiled up at me. One of the most torturous things I've ever done in my life was walk away that morning and leave Genevieve standing alone on the pier. Still, I treasured the sensation of the touch of her gaze on my back for the entire time it took me to stroll away.

Soon, I promised myself. I would see her again soon.

Galveston: 1900 A Storm, A Story of Twin Flames

CHAPTER 11

Genevieve's Diary: The Heart Locket

Locket with Uri's Photo Inside

5th June 1899

Yesterday was the loveliest day. Uri took me riding in his carriage. We stopped by the boardwalk just in front of Murdoch's and The Pagoda, and to my surprise, he reached into his coat pocket and pulled out of long black box. I opened it and found several gauzy layers of silk inside. Of course Uri thought it would be quite fun for me to spend so much time unwrapping his present. But it was worth the wait! He gave me breathtaking heart locket – I was utterly speechless. I opened it and saw a photograph of his handsome face looking back at me. As he clasped the exquisite necklace around my neck, he gave me a light kiss on the back of my neck and said, "You have my heart."

Of course, he has mine as well.

The necklace was unexpected and yet completely something that Uri would do. But he was full of surprises that night. He took us to dine at the fine restaurant located within The Tremont Hotel. Although the meal was most excellent – fish and scallops with wine – I couldn't help constantly touching his beautiful gift. Every time I did, Uri would place his hand over his heart, as if I was touching him directly.

It's strange, but I almost believe that I was. I could feel his heartbeat. And as it's his heart, I never want to part from it.

He is everything I ever wanted. Tall and athletic, his strong hands feel so reassuring in mine. I must not forget to mention how funny he can be, and how he can make me laugh.

Sadly, when I returned home, I had to remove it from my neck so as to avoid unnecessary questions from Mother. She wouldn't approve of Uri – although I don't understand why being Russian has anything to do with his character.

I don't understand her. She always seems hot under the collar. In the past she has never failed to remind me of the tortuous labor that almost killed her when I was born.

She seems to still blame me for not being able to have any more children. All I ever wanted from her was to care about me. I remember how disappointed I felt the day my teacher reported that I had even surpassed most of the boys in our school, in terms of mastery of the curriculum, and Mother failed to even to acknowledge this.

Still I will not let her spoil my present blessedness. I thank God for this very moment. It is worth a lifetime of heartache if this is the path that has led me to meet my dear Uri. There may be no coming atonement with Mother, but now I live with a different at-one-ment: with my beloved. I slept with the necklace under my pillow the entire night and dreamt of him. And as soon as I left this morning, I clasped the pendant back around my neck. Several of the children today told me how pretty it was, and wanted to know where I got it. Of course I didn't want to let on in front of the Sisters, but I couldn't help smiling when I said a certain guardian angel had given it to me. They very much liked that story. I shall have to bring Uri there one day to meet the children. They, of course, will be overjoyed to meet a true guardian angel. Just as I was.

Of course, as I returned home and reached the front door, I had to again remind myself not to let Mother see Uri's gift. I stopped and quickly unclasped the pendant and placed it carefully in my purse. It is Uri's heart, and I must be very good to it.

When I came inside, Mother was busy preparing dinner, so I stole a few moments to come up to my room and hid the necklace under my pillow. I rather enjoy the thought of sleeping next to Uri's heart. One day he will hopefully sleep next to mine.

Galveston: 1900 A Storm, A Story of Twin Flames

CHAPTER 12

Picnic on the Beach

Those early days spent with Genevieve are imprinted on my mind, the way her soul was engraved onto my own. The way her head tilted at each of my observations, or flew back as she laughed. The way the wind always tangled her wavy hair and the light caught her eyes. As I watched her, I finally understood that the wondrous, strange feeling inside me was the joined flame of our souls. I was, after so long, finally totally complete and whole.

This perception could not have been clearer than one day when we were enjoying a picnic on a secluded beach. I picked her up in my carriage in front of *The Beach Hotel*, her beaming smile lifting my heart. Leaving the front of the Hotel, I stopped at the large fountain on Beach Avenue so that my horse could have his fill of water before moving west on the esplanade. We passed *Murdoch's Bathhouse*, and then *Olympia* by the Sea, a three story circular structure complete with amusements, a restaurant, and a dance hall. I promised Genevieve that I would take her there soon at some future date.

Passing *O'Keefe's Bathhouse*, we now proceeded along the open trail in front of the beach as the warm Gulf breeze greeted our faces. She then rested her head on my shoulder. Everything was so perfect. My entire world seemed to vibrate with such perfection. Our hearts beat in unison as we rode on the path toward the Orphanage. Passing through the Midway, the stretch along the beach where rickety stores sold seashells, stereoscopic cards, and candy and where inexpensive restaurants served boiled clams and beer, we soon were out in the open where sand dunes covered with Morning Glory emerged to our left and where beyond that we could see the blue waters of the Gulf. To our right was the prairie interspersed with ponds and some live oaks. Even the seagulls that flew overhead seemed to feel our bliss as they lingered briefly before flying away.

Along the way she explained to me that the Orphanage was built away from the City in order to keep the children away from family members who had been infected during the Yellow Fever outbreak of more than 10 years ago. We continued traveling at our leisurely pace to a nice stretch of beach just ahead. I had known that this particular spot offered some privacy, and I wished to share it with Genevieve, who understood our need to give us our own place.

Upon arriving to this cloistered area of the Island, I tied the horse to a tree and helped Genevieve off the buggy. While she retrieved her purse, I gathered the picnic basket. With our free hand, we walked hand in hand over the green covered sand dune toward the water and saw a Rough-tailed Gecko scurry over the mound stirring up puffs of sand in its wake. Much later I had learned that in North America, the Rough-tailed Gecko could only be found on Galveston Island, having migrated on boats and ships from Africa and the Middle East.

A short distance later she squeezed my hand a little tighter and slowed the pace of her walk.

"Uri, wait a minute."

"Huh?"

"Look up ahead." She exclaimed, pointing to the sand seven yards ahead where a small mound with a myriad of indentations rested.

"It's a turtle nest!" She cooed.

" A nest?" I echoed.

"The momma turtle has laid her eggs there."

I now saw a trail of footprints that led to the edge of the water.

Sensing my perception she then continued. "When and where it's nice and quiet in the dead of the night, the female lays her eggs and returns to the sea before the dawn."

"I have swam amongst the turtles before… but I did not know where they were born. Where did you learn this?"

"One of the Mothers fancies these creatures. We have many nests around the Orphanage, being as secluded as we are. I have even seen the little ones hatch."

"Is that right." I said with fascination.

"They are so cute, Uri… breaking through their eggs and making a mad dash to the water." The excitement within her making her voice rise.

It was amazing how much life lived beneath the waves of the Gulf. It was like a virtual underwater forest, a body of water teeming with life. I remember not only swimming amongst green and hawksbill sea turtles but also with dolphins and fish of many different colors. The fish that darted within the warm waters of Galveston included striped mullet, black and red drum, and spotted sea trout. The dolphins would arrive in the spring and at times would be seen leaping out of the water.

We on the Island were also well versed to be wary of the occasional shark that would roam the currents following the trail of fish that comprised their diet. Fortunately, I never saw one of those predators, but I did have the knowledge of a young boy who had his hand bitten by a shark and was rushed to *Sealy Hospital* where his hand was amputated below the wrist. The Hospital, the first in Texas, had been named after John Sealy, the banker who established the *Galveston Wharf Company* and later who became owner of the *Buffalo Bayou, Brazos & Colorado Railway Company*.

What I had seen in person was the Texas Rattlesnake, a very common poisonous snake that turned out to be a very dangerous nuisance on the Island and in much of Texas. Accounts of Rattler bites and subsequent deaths were very common. My encounter with this pest occurred a number of years earlier when I was living with Peter, and I was cleaning the barn behind the house. As I was sweeping some leaves in the corner of the room, I heard its characteristic rattle and saw its tubular body scurry with great rapidity. It was a good five feet in length. Realizing that it would be best to have help, I fetched Peter and between the two of us, Peter with the pitchfork and me with the hoe, we were able to kill the repulsive animal.

Genevieve and I now carefully stepped around the delicate mound, and soon I found the perfect patch of sand where I pitched the picnic blanket. We took out the sandwiches, potato salad, and bottle of wine and began eating.

We sat relaxing on a large picnic blanket, our meal finished, enjoying the ocean breeze even as the bright sun beat down on us. We were both dressed casually – she in a light blue muslin dress and me in a white cotton shirt and linen pants. As was our way, we were jumping from topic to topic in our conversation, letting the words that seemed to flow like the tide takes us where they willed.

"It was Peter's idea to come to America. Peter vowed not to live the life of our Father."

"And what is that?" She inquired. Her eyes squinting slightly as the angle of the sun was now catching them.

I shrugged at her.

"He is a farmer. Peter and I would help him plant the crops in the spring and harvest them in the fall. Taking care of the animals in the winter was the worst. It was so miserably cold. Your breath would freeze in mid air." I remarked while gesturing with my hand in front of my mouth.

"That's hard to imagine."

We both shared a laugh as a strong gust from the waves fanned our bodies, helping to combat the Texas heat. Frozen Russia was truly another world in that moment.

"As difficult as it was for her, Mother encouraged both of us to leave. She wished us a better life. We now send money home so that Father does not have to work so hard."

"But… why don't they come here?" I let out a sigh.

"Father is set in his ways. He would have a hard time adapting to a new lifestyle in a different country – especially in such a hot one!"

We laughed again.

As I paused in reflection, my eyes drifted to the waters of the Gulf where a steamship was crossing the horizon on its way to the docks on the Bay side of the Island.

"I'm not the only one who has obstacles to overcome. After all, it must be challenging to deal with the children at the Orphanage."

"Freud helps." She asserted confidently.

It was my turn to look at her in surprise.

"Sigmund Freud?"

She looked at me as if I was slow.

"Yes, Sigmund Freud. I read his books."

The smile on my face stilled as I looked at her.

"The mind also." I said softly.

"What?"

The breeze once again picked up and started to tangle her wavy hair. My hand stole across her brow, down the side of her head, and down her hair.

"Your mind is also so beautiful." I affirmed quietly as close to one another as we were.

She looked at me solemnly, smiling with only her eyes, and I knew in that moment she loved me totally and completely as much as I loved her.

Suddenly, her eyes widened.

"I have something for you!"

Genevieve dived for her purse and pulled out two thick books. I hadn't realized she was carrying such a heavy bag. With a flourish, she presented them to me.

"For you. They are the latest editions."

As I reached out to take the books, my eyes finally registered their titles – **Outline of Pharmacology** by Schmiedeberg and ***A Treatise on Anatomy and Physiology***, **and** ***Hygiene*** by Cutter. She knew and appreciated my passion for science, and my research and studies at the *Medical College.*

"Oh my…" I exclaimed with delight.

My hands traced the leather covers reverently.

"For the great scientist inside you. Never give up your dreams." She declared with great sincerity and conviction.

Before she could settle back, I reached out to grab her hand and place it on top of the books, my hand covering hers. Everything that was most vital to my being was held there in the space of my hand. My heart quickened, as I was about to say something that for some time needed to be expressed.

"Back in Russia some of our people study an ancient philosophy of mystics. There are anecdotes about the soul that say before we are born, our soul is whole and in unison with the Creator."

I lay the books down, and then tenderly put her hand against my chest.

"At birth, half of our soul is separated. When we find our twin flame, our soul becomes whole again, restored to the perfection that it once had." I leaned my head closer, the fragrance of her hair and skin consuming my senses.

"You make everything so perfect." I whispered.

Slowly, my eyes locked on hers. Spellbound by her being, I brought my lips down to meet hers. In that first gentle kiss, all of my dreams became real, within reach. I felt rapture in the heat of her adoration. Genevieve now circled her arms around my neck and rested her head against my chin.

"Uri… you have my heart. It is with you always, since the moment we met." She susurrated in my ear.

She now leaned slightly back to look into my eyes and clasped the locket I'd given her tightly in one fist. She consumed me with her captivating eyes.

"I love you." She affirmed with total certainty.

Once again, I placed her other hand against my heart.

"And I love you."

Those words released a rush of passion, making my heartbeat faster.

We needed no more words in that moment. I was hers and she was mine. She leaned into me, and we shared a long, tender kiss. I cradled her in my arms, and we remained that way, eyes closed, for a long time unwilling to let the moment pass, soaking up each other's very presence. Feeling the absolute certainty of the rightness of our declarations.

At last, I opened my eyes and looked out over the water. The sun was beginning to set, and the June bugs were beginning to chorus. The sky was a stunning palate of swirling orange, magenta, and lavender, and the water was catching some of these amazing hues.

"Genevieve, what do you think the water is like?" I playfully asked.

She sat up slowly.

"You mean get in the water?" She asked with some surprise.

She looked at me and I flashed her a mischievous smile.

"Yes!"

"I didn't bring my bathing suit."

I unfolded my legs and stood up.

"It doesn't matter."

Laughing, I started running toward the water.

"I'll race you in." I said, challenging her to follow me.

Genevieve got up.

"Uri…" She countered with a little bit of protest in her voice.

"Come on!" I shouted encouragingly.

I ran into the water until it was shin deep. Shrieks echoed behind me as Genevieve followed my lead and waded into the surf. As she came to meet me, I reached out and pulled her into an embrace. She was laughing, her head back, and I joined in, whirling her around and getting us thoroughly soaked.

After a few moments, our laughter gradually faded. We stared, mesmerized by the look in each other's eyes. The world around us melted away – there was no setting sun or breaking waves or calling gulls. There were only us, united in a singular moment of eternal time.

In that moment, I leaned down and again gently kissed Genevieve. But the tenderness faded as she reached for me and I pulled her tightly against me. Our kisses deepened as our passion for each other began to overflow. Everything else faded as only the sensation of rapturous adoration remained, intensifying with each passing second. We were conveyed, it seemed, to another dimension, where the only important thing that existed in the whole Universe was our love for each other.

Suddenly, a large wave crashed around us, tugging us back to the world of the beach, sweeping us off our feet. But we didn't fight the tide. Instead, we let it deposit us against the sand. Uninterrupted, we continued kissing passionately as we lay in shallow water, covered in sand and salt, refusing to let go of one another.

Just as the sunlight started to fade, we reluctantly pulled away. The wind was turning chilly and I didn't want Genevieve to catch a cold. I stood up and turned to help her to her feet. A soft smile, full of satisfaction, lit her face, drops of saltwater dripping down her cheeks. My hands caressed the planes of her face, memorizing every detail.

"I don't ever want to be without you."

She said nothing, only reached up and pulled my head down and placed my lips against hers. There we stood. Both of us undivided. A unitary soul, alone on a beach. Mindless of anything else but our being, and I knew I would hold and cherish her inside of me as long as I lived.

CHAPTER 13

Hank

Little did I know that a storm was brewing behind us as we rode off in my buggy and back to the city. It came in the form of a clap of thunder that I heard as we were riding along Bath Avenue, accompanied by the form of Mr. Hank Ottenburg hitting the street with his bag of tools.

Had I glanced back, I might have seen the rage filled face as he realized that the object of his affections was intimately involved with someone else, her head lovingly resting on my shoulder. I might have seen him fling his bag to the ground and kick it while muttering obscenities. I might have seen Dr. Young, who later informed of what I had missed seeing, glancing at Hank in consternation even as thunder crashed down out of the sky. But I looked only forward, my joy forming a willful barrier of ignorance as enormous thunderheads formed over the Bay. The storm couldn't hurt me- hurt us- safe as we were in each other's love.

It was the end of another work-filled evening a few days after Genevieve and I rode away from the storm. It had blown itself out, and so had any questions I had about the rightness of our courtship, our love. I returned to my work and my studies renewed, and threw myself into the business at hand. Peter and I were nearly always the last two in the shop at the end of the day, and so it was that evening. Peter had already finished getting ready for the next day, but I was still at the counter writing notes in the business log.

Hat in hand, Peter walked to the door then turned to address me.

"Well, I'm ready. Will you be much longer?"

I shook my head at my brother.

"Go ahead. I'll finish shortly." I responded, absentmindedly, engrossed as I was with my notes.

"Very well. I will see you tomorrow."

Again, an absent nod from me.

"Horosho (okay)." He asserted as he placed his hat on his head.

Peter left the shop, the jangling bell ringing hollowly throughout the empty building. Shortly thereafter, I put the logbook away and checked my desk for any lingering work I might have missed. My eyes caught on the books that Genevieve gave me.

I looked at them longingly; touching them lightly and feeling a smile steal across my face at the memory of how Genevieve had presented them to me. With a sigh, I turned away, gathered my hat and keys, shut off the lights, and walked out the front door.

After walking outside and locking the shop securely, I turned the corner and started to walk pass a darkened alley. As I started moving past it, a voice slithered out from the darkness.

"Hey.... Uri."

Startled, I paused, unable to locate the source of the voice or recognize its origin. Its Southern drawl and unfriendly tone connected me to a flash of thought- Culture of Honor. Out of the shadowy corner emerged a young man, looking somewhat inebriated. He almost looked familiar, but it wasn't until he spoke that I realized who he was.

"I want you to stay away from Genevieve." There was anger in his voice.

"Who are you?"

"The name is Hank."

Understanding dawned on my face. Genevieve had told me of her unwanted, would-be suitor, and a lout named Hank that she absolutely abhorred. He had, it seemed, discovered my romance with Genevieve.

"She's not your girl."

Hank took a threatening step towards me, coming within striking distance. His fists clenched at his sides, even as he drunkenly swayed on his feet.

"I guess you didn't hear what I said, Russian boy, so lemme say it again: stay away from her."

I shook my head at him.

"I do not need to listen to this."

I turned to leave, but before I could do so, Hank put his hand on my shoulder, spun me to face him, and punched me across the face. The blow was sharp and my face immediately began throbbing, but I recovered quickly and began throwing numerous punches at him.

I was a fairly decent fighter, but Hank seemed to absorb my punches with little effect, the alcohol serving to strengthen his rage. But I was quicker than he, my reflexes faster. After landing several more punches, I finally gained the advantage. I threw a right across his face and followed it with two body shots to the stomach. Hank crumpled to the ground, gasping. I stopped, my breath also coming short, and leaned over him.

"You bastard," he ground out.

In a blink, Hank grabbed a handful of dirt and threw it into my eyes. Stunned, I staggered back as Hank rose to his feet and started viciously punching me everywhere – stomach, chest, face. The dirt clung to my eyes, erasing my vision and any hope of defending myself. Pain blossomed across my body as I belatedly sought to protect myself, my eyes forgotten. Hank finally punched me across the eye, and I fell to the ground, dazed. I felt a final hard kick across the head, leaving me semiconscious and unable to move. Agony burned throughout my body, and my head threatened to split open. Blood poured out of my nose and a sharp pain across my chest told me my lungs were likely damaged as well. Before I passed out completely, I felt Hank spit on my battered and bloodied body.

"You carpetbaggers need to get back to your own country."

My last thought was of my poor Genevieve. How could I protect her from a beast like Hank, if I couldn't even defend myself?

CHAPTER 14

Genevieve's Diary: The Evening of the Assault

15th June 1899

Oh, that dreadful, vile, horrible man! Mother will be waiting the rest of her life if she thinks I will ever have anything to do with someone like him. He should be sentenced and locked up, but I fear he will get away with it. And Mother... what will I do?

What a horrid night!

I was at St. Mary's Orphanage last evening, working with the nuns to take care of the children as I usually do. It's a rather depressing building – two stories high but crammed with almost a hundred children.

I was sitting in the dining table with the young Mother Superior, Camillus Tracy (only 30!), and the other nine sisters who run the orphanage. They were finishing up their meals, but I found I had no appetite. I was uneasy and restless, a feeling that had plagued me throughout the day. Only now it was an overwhelming certainty.

Something was wrong.

My hands crept up to touch the heart locket that Uri gave, hanging serenely around my neck. As I clasped it, an image rose in my mind – Uri's face, concerned... then afraid.

I stood up abruptly. Sister Tracy looked at me in alarm.

"What is it?"

"It's just that –" I hesitated; unsure of how to explain the growing belief inside me that Uri was in danger.

"No... I must leave now, Sister Tracy." Without a second glance, I rushed out of the room.

I don't remember much of my trip across town. Panic pushed me forward, blinding, thoughtless haste mixed with fear at what I'd find. Moments later, I turned a corner near Uri's shop. In the distance, I saw Uri crumpled on the dirt. I ran to his side, sobbing with dread.

"No, no. God, please, no…"

I gathered Uri protectively in my arms, relieved to find him breathing. Even though it was getting dark outside, I screamed for help, sure that someone would find us. After only a few minutes, several people arrived, and we were carted off to the Medical College.

I stayed with him that entire night, certain that my presence was helping him, because he knew I was there. His brother arrived later, and after the doctors pronounced him stable in the early morning hours, it was decided that Uri be sent home. I hovered in the background, unsure of what to do. But Uri, who had finally regained consciousness, whispered my name.

"Genevieve."

I went to his side, fighting to hide the sobs that wanted to break out of my lungs. He was a mess. His eyes were black and his entire face was swollen and covered with cuts and abrasions.

"Why? Why would anyone do this to you?"

He looked up at me, anguish in his eyes, then looked away, unwilling to answer. But I knew. I could see it in his eyes. It was someone who wanted my love, but I had denied. And so he went after his competition, somehow convinced that would win me over.

Hank – that deceitful, hateful, waste of a man!

I stayed with Uri all of the next day, even though he mostly slept, before he woke late in the afternoon and finally convinced me that I needed to go home before Mother had a fit, as she had no idea where I was. I reluctantly agreed, though I knew he was now safe.

"I will come see you tomorrow, my love."

He smiled at me, a small smile, all that his beloved and torn face could handle.

"I will dream of you until then."

On the way home, my thoughts were consumed with the pain of knowing that Hank had not only found out about Uri and me, he had also nearly killed him. Something had to be done. But when I finally arrived home, there was even more bad news to be heard.

Mother was waiting in the living. The opening of the front door literally caught her pacing back and forth in agitation. Still, I was a little surprised to see her waiting there.

"Mother?" She turned to face me fully.

"We need to talk. Where were you last night?"

I remained silent, unsure of how to begin to explain.

"You were with that Russian man from the print shop." She said it with accusing certainty.

So she knew.

"Yes." What I didn't realize was how furious she was that I was seeing a man from Russia. Her prejudice made her blind.

"Damn it. How could you do this to me? I prohibited you from seeing him. What will people think? He is a foreigner for God's sake." Still, hearing those words out of her mouth – the curses, the disgust, and the petty hate – it was too much. I started crying, hurt beyond words at Mother's behavior.

"His name is Uri, Mother. Uri Petrakov. And I don't care what others think." She whirled away, hands flying in the air as she gesticulated angrily.

"You don't care? Proper families follow certain standards. What kind of Christian is he?"

"I don't know. His parents are Greek Orthodox." She turned to face me again, her face mottled red.

"Greek Orthodox? That's no Christian." Mother grabbed a framed certificate sitting on top of the buffet. It was my "Certificate of Baptism."

"You see this? You are different. Your values are not like his."

I wanted to explain, to tell her what Hank had done to Uri, what hate had done to him. But all that came out was how I felt about Uri.

"I value love, and I love him." Mother froze.

"What did you say?" The tone of her voice should have warned me, but after the attack on Uri and her unthinking malice, I refused to heed that warning. I recklessly pledged my love to Uri.

"I love him, and nothing on this Earth can change that." Quicker than a thought, Mother slapped me hard across the face. Stunned, it took a moment for the pain to register. When it did, I started to cry, deep sobs of disbelief shaking my body.

"Love? You don't even know what love is. I forbid you from seeing that man again. If you see him again, I will throw you out of this house."

Defiance roared out of my mouth. "I'm ready to leave now." I turned to walk away, out of the house, but Mother's words stopped me in my tracks.

"Then I will shoot him myself. My daughter will not be disrespected by hell-bound Russian trash."

Mother left the room, the door slamming shut behind her. But I didn't leave. How could I? I would rather die than see any harm come to Uri. I can't bear to live through another night like the previous one.

I sank onto the sofa, sobbing inconsolably, utterly alone with my pain and torment.

Mother hated Uri. Hated him without knowing him at all. She'd hurt him if I left. And Hank... he'd already hurt Uri. All I wanted to do was love him, but it seems as if I will only bring him pain.

But I know what to do now. How to make it better... for Uri. For everyone.

Galveston: 1900 A Storm, A Story of Twin Flames

Galveston: 1900 A Storm, A Story of Twin Flames

CHAPTER 15

Recuperating

The First Hospital in Texas, John Sealy Hospital

Courtesy of Texas State Library & Archives Commission

The details of the night of the beating remain sketchy because of the concussion I had suffered. I vaguely recall being carted to *Sealy Hospital* and undergoing x-rays with the newly invented x-ray machine. The x-rays showed some cracked ribs. My abrasions where cleaned and some stitches were also administered. I also recollect Peter's face looking down at me and for a moment, I had a flash back to the accident when I fell through the ice. The one thing that I surely remember, even in the fog of semi-consciousness, was that Genevieve was there with me the entire time. Throughout the ordeal I could feel her concern and love.

I was released in the early morning hours and once at home, slept most of the rest of the next day. Genevieve, having accompanied me, periodically applied ice to my swollen face. When I became more cognizant, I realized that her Mother would be worried and insisted she go back home.

"Mary will take care of me while you are gone."

"Are you sure? I don't want to leave you." She said, eyes full of sorrow.

"I'm an indestructible Russian." I replied with a faint smile.

"I'll be fine here with Mary taking care of me, besides we don't need any more drama."

"O.K., but I will be back tomorrow." She reluctantly agreed.

The following morning I awoke to the early golden rays of a June dawn, head and body aching. Something had been ruminating within my thoughts ever since that night of the attack. As I lay on my bed, the word "Carpet baggers", uttered with all its scorn and hate, emerged. My thoughts turned to what it meant to be an immigrant in my new home. This land of opportunity also had presented its challenges. Not only the need to learn a different language and adapt to a new culture, but to find acceptance from some of those who were already here. Immigrants were viewed, for the most part, as laborers for factories and construction. We were the artisans with the skill to bring architectural beauty to the urban landscape. To have established such a successful business, such as the one Peter and I owned, was to disturb what the establishment considered the natural order of things. It brought out, in some, resentment and envy.

In the America of the late 19th century, there definitely was a social order with the Anglo American unrivaled, at the very top. The Anglo immigrant then followed. Below that was the Jew. Interacting with a Jew was foreign to me. I did not know any Jews back in Russia, although I had heard of this group and of the pogroms, unprovoked raids on Jewish communities, which were often carried out in certain areas of Russia. Here in Galveston there was a small Jewish community that worshipped at

B'nai Israel with its distinction of being the first Jewish congregation in Texas. I recalled, now and then, overhearing comments that the Jews were greedy Christ killers whom were all going to hell. These comments puzzled me as I remembered that Jesus himself was Jewish and forgave and loved even his enemies. The Jews I had met here in Galveston seemed to me to be devoted, industrious people.

The unfavorable view in the eyes of many toward the Jew, however, paled in comparison to the widespread hate for the colored people. I heard many openly call them "stupid and lazy niggards". I remembered an Old Timer saying "You ain't nothing if you can't be better than a niggard." almost spitting out the word "niggard." This saying seemed to show that there were those who needed someone beneath them to assure themselves of their own superiority. I later learned that the Old Timer had participated in Pickett's Charge at the Battle of Gettysburg. He would never accept The Emancipation Proclamation, and he still believed that "The South Will Rise Again."

The very idea that some people were stupid and also hated only because of their skin color troubled me. I recall having read some of the speeches written by Frederick Douglass. These speeches argued for freedom and justice and for truly embracing the American-born concept that all men were created equal. Douglass' writings seemed, to me, to be on par with those of the great President Lincoln, the master orator whose winged words could move mountains of bigotry.

The hatred for the colored people had been indoctrinated into Southern Society by the passing of *Jim Crow Laws*, laws that had established the creation of separate but unequal facilities such as restrooms, railroad passenger coaches, and schools. These laws also impeded the right to vote by imposing poll taxes and "literacy tests." The colored people lived in the glum shadows of society, toiling in the most undesirable types of labor, such as cleaning outhouses, picking up trash, toiling in the hot fields. They lived in shantytowns on the outskirts of the towns and cities. Their children were taught in ramshackle buildings that were called "schools." I saw the colored people and felt their pain.

Grimacing as I turned on my side, I also thought how I finally had come face to face with "The Culture of Honor". I was a "carpetbagger, a foreigner" who had usurped what was not rightfully his. "The Culture of Honor" was a phenomenon that was particularly prevalent amongst Southerners that held that the defense of one's honor was not only an obligation but also a great act of nobility. I had seen fights at some of the local saloons erupt for some of the most inconsequential reasons, such as someone looking at another "the wrong way' or questioning someone's word as a man.

    We indeed stood at the dawn of a new century, marvelous with technological and scientific progress. This advances had so vastly changed the world that even what was known a mere seventy-five years earlier seemed like ancient history. The world was becoming a much smaller place, connected by transatlantic telegraph, newspaper reporting, and international mail. Our humanity, however, still had a long way to go.

    Mary now cheerfully entered my room, carrying a tray with coffee and French toast. I sat up to eat, and as I had breakfast, my thoughts turned to Genevieve. She would be here soon. That anticipation alone made me feels better, evaporating the somber, unpleasant thoughts that had clouded my mind that morning. Only she could ever have such a healing effect on me.

CHAPTER 16

At the Print Shop

A number of days later after having been nursed back to health by Genevieve, I went back to work. I had had an odd, uneasy feeling ever since the night of the beating, one of impending dread. Till that night I had attributed that feeling to the after effects of the injuries I had sustained.

That day Genevieve stopped by the Shop to see me. We retreated to the office for some privacy while Peter over saw the business.

"How are you feeling, my Darling?" She said subdued, head tilted in observation, tender concern filling her eyes.

"Better… I'm starting to look like myself."

I sensed some woefulness about her.

"What's wrong?"

"I've been worried about you… What Hank did… It's just that I don't ever want anything to ever happen to you."

"Nothing is going to happen. I am Russian and indestructible." I playfully added.

"Sure…" She gave a small smile as she gently touched the side of my swollen face.

"Besides soon when we marry, we will always be together."

I reached out and caressed her hair.

"Nothing will make me happier… You are my light." She affirmed.

Taking her by the hand I suggested.

"Let me take you home."

"No you have a lot of work to finish."

"I do… but it can wait. Please…"

"I can't right now." She now seemed to force a smile. " You know Mother. She's a strange bird. How many ladies do you know that own guns?"

"I don't care. Sooner or later I'll have to face her." I stated with some annoyance rising in my voice.

Genevieve remained unmoved, unconvinced.

"Then I'll meet you at the Orphanage tomorrow?" I offered.

"Yes."

We shared a kiss tender, but with a sense of sorrow. We exited the office and I watched her walk out the front door.

Galveston: 1900 A Storm, A Story of Twin Flames

CHAPTER 17

Genevieve's Diary: No Way Out

Full Moon Over The Gulf of Mexico

25th June 1899

It is now the morning after the most horrendous day of my life. Thank God things will be much better now.

I saw no other way to fix the dilemma that Uri and me were in. I knew what that Witch was truly capable of. She would shoot him if that what it took, and with him being a foreigner, may have even gotten away with murder.

I had visited with Uri that very day while he was working at the Print Shop. He wanted to take me home, to face Mother. How could I have told him that she threatened to kill him, after everything he had been through? He promised to meet me at the Orphanage the next day. We kissed before I left, my heart breaking. I tried my best to hide my feelings from him, but he knows me all too well. Somehow I managed to hold the tears till I was outside the Shop.

I knew Mother would not be home that evening as she had gone to Church to finish a quilt for a Church fundraiser with some of the Church ladies. Father was in San Antonio on duty with the Railroad.

I composed a letter to my Love, my Life, explaining what I felt I had to do. I told him that I could never let any harm come to him. I explained to him that Mother was a bitter, hateful person who would never let us be together. I told him that he must go on afterward. I would always be near; no one had ever or could bring the joy that he had into my life.

That night I walked the short distance to The Beach Hotel and then to The Pagoda Bathhouse. Being mid week, I was completely alone. I walked up the pier and at the very spot were Uri and I had talked that first time. I took off my shoes and placed the note in one of them. I then retraced my steps and walked down to the beach.

The full moon overhead lit the tops of the waves. I closed my eyes holding my locket that was around my neck in my fist. The swishing sound of the Gulf seemed to beckon me. I stepped into the warm water and preceded slowly, my only thoughts on Uri. As I had reached waist deep level water, I heard a shout from behind me.

"Genevieve!" It was Mother and she had waded into the water a number of yards behind me.

"Oh it's you. Leave me alone. Don't come any closer." I was surprised and disgusted that somehow she had found me.

"My baby, what are you doing?" I could hear desperation in her voice.

"Go away!" You won't have to worry about a daughter disgracing the family name."

"My darling, don't do it. You are my only child. Don't break my heart."

"You don't care about breaking mine. Uri is my life. That Hank that you admire so much beat him senseless the other night. He almost killed him."

"Oh my God." I was surprised to hear some concern coming out of that heartless mouth.

"Uri is my life. I don't want to live without him and I won't." I then moved out further into the water.

Mother followed me, crying and pleading. "Please my Darling, come back. Don't do it. Think of Papa. Don't break his heart. I know I have been wrong. I promise to be more opened minded about Uri. I will do whatever you want. Please give me chance, Genevieve, I beg of you." She was desperately pleading through pained sobs.

Now thinking of Papa, and of Mother's seeming sincerity and her promise to let Uri and me be, I stopped. I felt her arms wrap around me, and I turned around. We both cried and then embraced in each other's arms.

As she took me by the hand, my thoughts immediately turned to my Uri.

I could some how feel his eyes upon me. As we walked out of the surf, I saw, in the far distance, a figure running toward me. Sure enough it was he, and having somehow known that I was in danger, he had come to save me.

Galveston: 1900 A Storm, A Story of Twin Flames

CHAPTER 18

A Premonition

For the entire remainder of the day that Genevieve had stopped at the Shop, the queasiness at the pit of my stomach remained. I attributed it to the lingering effects of my injuries and after work went home where I had a very light meal. Feeling poorly, I turned in very early and drifted into an unsettled, light sleep. No sooner had this happened than I saw a type of dream, but strangely unlike any other dream I had had before. It was more of a vision. Through a mist of fog, I saw Genevieve's face directly in front of mine, pained and streaked with tears. Her face, filled with morn and regret, now started slowly to drift away from me.

Immediately, I awoke in a full panic, and hopped into my shoes. I dashed downstairs through the front door and finding my horse in the stables slapped the saddle on him. Hell bent, I rode to the one place that had come into my mind: *The Bath House.*

With the full moon illuminating the way, I soon was at the beach where I jumped off my horse and ran toward two figures that were walking out of the water's edge. As I approached Genevieve, her Mother stood frozen where she was. We collapsed into each other's arms, waves of relief overcoming me, knowing that my Genevieve was now safe.

She then informed her Mother that she would be home later and would further discuss matters at that time. Her Mother looked at me with guilty awkwardness, but I said nothing as I placed my hand on her shoulder and led Genevieve away. Soaking wet I placed her on the horse and then mounted the horse myself, riding behind her. I then took her to the Villa where I wrapped her in a warm blanket and prepared for her some tea. She told me everything that had happened. I was horrified, absolutely sickened, to realize how close I was to losing her. But from what she informed me regarding her Mother, I now saw that the one obstacle that had kept us from being together was now gone.

Galveston: 1900 A Storm, A Story of Twin Flames

CHAPTER 19

Getting Permission

Edwardian Beauty

After that incident, I had a lengthy visit with Mr. and Mrs. Parker asking their permission for Genevieve's hand in marriage. Mr. Parker, tall and lean with weathered skin from working so many hours outdoors, was quite pleasant. I could tell by the way he said things how very much he loved his daughter. Mrs. Parker, on the other hand, was only politely businesslike, which suited me fine. It was the most I could have expected from her.

I professed my love for Genevieve and promised to cherish and care for her always. When they expressed their concern regarding our having different religions, I immediately said that I would convert to Catholicism.

The first thing I had to do was buy Genevieve a ring. I went to every jewelry store on the Island before finding the perfect one, a Dida Edwardian beauty. The central European cut diamond was a full carat and a half. Accent diamonds and swirling milgrain detail as well as chevron cutouts surrounded this central diamond. When I presented it to her at her home, Genevieve lost her breath, taken aback at such a beautiful ring.

I began conversions classes immediately, attending classes three times a week at *St. Mary's Cathedral School* located on 20th and Winnie Street. *St. Mary's Cathedral*, where we were to marry, was just across the street. Classes were quite lengthy and I found the rituals elaborate and interesting.

There was much, however, I did not understand as the Mass was conducted in Latin. That puzzled me as I had thought that Aramaic, the language of Jesus, would have been much more appropriate. Nonetheless, I did not raise any questions, as in those days, dogma had to be accepted on pure faith and could not be scrutinized.

What I did relish the most was that I could court Genevieve in the open with no worry of someone seeing us and reporting back to Mrs. Parker. We would often go to *Olympia* by The Sea, the three-story circular entertainment complex, located west of *The Beach Hotel*. *Olympia* featured a restaurant with a magnificent view of the Gulf on the third floor, and a dance hall on the second floor. The first floor was filled with shops where for a fee one could see 3-D stereopticons, take photographs, and play darts. It also housed a marvelous candy store where even the air smelled sweet and delicious, and where you could buy all sorts of sweets including Cracker Jacks, Hershey Chocolate Bars, and Fig Newtons.

It was, however, the *Olympia's* second floor dance hall where Genevieve and I would most often frequent. At least once a week, we would listen and dance to splendid music. Our favorite dances were two stepping to *"Maple Leaf Rag"* and *"She'll be coming Around the Mountain."* We also danced cheek to cheek to *"Carry Me Back to Old*

Virginia" and *"I'll take you home Again, Kathleen."*

Although the *Olympia* had a mostly younger crowd, it also had its share of Old Timers. These older couples would often request the band to play the *Schottische*, a dance in which couples gracefully traveled in a circle. It was so different from the Russian Folk Dances I had seen in my youth. Those dances, though starting slowly like the *Schottische*, accelerated greatly in tempo as the song progressed. The Russian dance had much foot stomping and flared kicks and turns, as well as deep knee bending moves by the male dancers. It was interesting to me to see how dancing was evolving; from very patterned, rigid choreography to the more individualistic forms of the two-step. It dawned on me that the changes in dance seemed to reflect the evolving societal structure of conformity, moving to more individual freedom.

The liveliest and most popular song that was requested by the Old Timers was *"Dixie."* The male Old Timers were particularly invigorated by this music as it reminded them of their youth during the Civil War. As the song ended many of them would be hooting and hollering like mad men. They called that *"The Rebel Yell"*. By the end of the song, Genevieve and I would merely look at each other, not knowing what to say at the entertaining, silliness that we were observing. She would then throw her head backward, ebullient with laughter with me also following suit.

Those certainly were the most fond of days.

Galveston: 1900 A Storm, A Story of Twin Flames

CHAPTER 20

Genevieve's Diary: The Ring & The Fourth of July

4th July, 1899 The Band Playing "The Star Spangled Banner" at The Beach Hotel

30th June 1899

Oh my Lord! What a beautiful ring Uri gave me. I have never seen one like it. Mother, of course, downplayed the engagement ring. She seemed a little jealous, but that won't spoil the happiness I feel. I will wear his ring proudly and so look forward to the day we will marry and be together.

5th July 1899

Such a lovely holiday! Uri and I celebrated the 4th of July at The Beach Hotel. He picked me up from home, and we rode to the Hotel where we enjoyed a delicious lunch: tuna salad, carrots and peas, corn bread, and home made apple pie a la mode, for desert. After lunch we went to the front lawn to see the high wire act.

The acrobat was quite brave, fifty feet in the air with no net underneath. I held my breath a few times and clutched Uri tightly when the dare devil seemed to be in danger of losing his balance. Never the less, he made it fine.

After the high wire act, the band played "The Star Spangled Banner" and "America the Beautiful." As afternoon turned to evening, dance music filled the air. There were so many people there. Uri and I danced to our hearts content. I could have danced with him forever. I daresay that we even stole some kisses while on the dance floor. The night was capped by a marvelous fireworks display and more kisses for Uri.

Galveston: 1900 A Storm, A Story of Twin Flames

CHAPTER 21

At the Beach Hotel

The Beach Hotel

The first 4th of July that I shared with Genevieve was one I will never forget. Peter and I worked many extra hours the week before the holiday and having all our orders up to date, we were able to close three extra days. While I would stay on the Island to spend time with Genevieve, Peter, Karina and the children would travel via train to San Antonio where they would stay at *The Menger Hotel* and visit *The Alamo* next door to the Hotel.

I had learned that *The Beach Hotel* was planning a sensational July 4th evening filled with entertainment and music. Arriving at the hotel, a wooden four-story Victorian structure painted in brilliant carmine, olive and pale green, the grounds were filled with a multitude of celebrants. We made our way through the lobby past the billiards hall, the saloon where lively groups were drinking and playing poker, and walking up the Grand Staircase passed the reading room where we finally arrived at the dining room.

We were seated in the bay window area under the large dome. From the windows, we could see the beach, the Gulf and *Pagoda*. The day was cloudless and hot, just below us was the hotel gazebo and beyond that a beach filled with bathers and many rolling bathhouses; small structures that were wheeled onto the beach were people could change clothes in private. Swimmers dotted the water around *The Pagoda* like ants in a pond.

After lunch, we made our way to the front lawn where we enjoyed a high wire act followed by dancing on a platform that had been set up by the hotel. As light of the day began to fade, the hotel staff turned on the outside lights, both electric and gas, irradiating the building like a Christmas tree.

We danced the night away immersed in each other's arms, captivated in each other's presence. We two stepped to *"Maple Leaf Rag"* and *"I've Been Working on the Railroad."* When the band played *"Amazing Grace"*, we slow danced cheek to cheek and looking deeply into each other's eyes broke a taboo by kissing there on the dance floor. We swayed to the music, feet seeming to float above the dance floor.

At around 9:00 p.m., everybody was directed to the back, beach side of the Hotel, for the fireworks show. A stupendous display was presented in exploding lights of red, white, and blue.

The discharge of light illuminated the back verandas of the hotel and turned the night sky to day. The sparkles that cascaded down from the sky reflected on the waves of the Gulf like confetti on foamy water. In the midst of cheering revelers and the boom of the exploding fireworks again we kissed, so filled with the elation of having each other and sharing

this enchanted moment.
  That was the final time we spent at that Hotel. It burned to the ground the following month, leaving nothing more than supporting stilts and its immense brick chimney sticking out, like a gravestone.

Galveston: 1900 A Storm, A Story of Twin Flames

CHAPTER 22

Holidays

24th December 1899

Between the time I spent with Genevieve, research, working at the Shop, my conversion classes, and planning our wedding the rest of the year through the time of the our wedding seemed to pass as one big blur. As busy as I was, however, I never felt tired for just being in her presence invigorated me with seemingly boundless energy. That December, Genevieve and I welcomed Christmas by decorating the house with a Christmas tree as well as by hanging balls of mistletoe from the ceiling. Together we went shopping and bought gifts for our family and friends. Included with the gifts were baskets filled with oranges and grapefruits. In those days, citrus fruits were a rare treat that were mainly available for the holidays as transportation by train from Florida made year round availability of those treats prohibitive.

As for the gifts she gave me, Genevieve took the time to make two pairs of exquisite hand mittens, and she also embroidered six handkerchiefs. I gave her a superb evening dress made of white satin and silk overlay. The dress was also adorned with red accents and came with a matching plumed hat. For Christmas dinner, we were invited to Peter's. Genevieve prepared a tasty wassail bowl, a hot beverage made with cider and spiced with cinnamon and nutmeg. She also brought plum pudding that she had prepared herself. The dish was a baked aromatic spicy dessert made with raisins, nuts and apples that were shaped like inverted teacups.

I remember the excitement and anticipation that most of us felt as the New Century approached. My Princess and I so looked forward to marrying in April. Mingled with the expectation was an anxiety amongst some who believed that the End of Times was upon us. They sincerely presumed that the world was somehow going to end and that The Rapture would come to save the fortunate few. The New Century, of course, rolled around without incident.

Genevieve and I welcomed the New Century by attending festivities that included dinner, dancing and fireworks at Olympia by the Sea. At midnight all the gaslights were extinguished and each couple was given a candle that we each lit. Amidst the glow of candlelight, the band played *To Auld Lang Syne*, and the entire gathering joined in chorus.

For our first Valentine's Day, I created a unique card. As was the custom of the time, it was a three dimensional card on a base composed of a cylindrical honeycomb paper matrix that opened to form the base of the card. On top of this base was another honeycomb paper matrix that opened to form a heart. On a paper template outlining the shape of the heart, I wrote "I Love You Forever. Happy Valentine's Day!"

Genevieve gave me a delicious chocolate cake with strawberry filling shaped in a heart that she baked herself. My Princess was blessed with so many talents and baking was certainly one of them.

That evening we attended a concert at *Harmony Hall*, a spacious Renaissance style structure located on Church Street, one block east of *The Tremont* where we enjoyed a marvelous concert in which the debut of the song " I Love You Truly" was sung. I remember the lyrics and melody as though I heard them yesterday.

" I love you truly, truly dear.
Life with its sorrow, life with its tears
Fades into dreams when I feel you are near
For I love you truly, truly dear…"
"Ah! Love, 'tis something to feel your kind hand
Ah! Yes, tis something by your side to stand;
Gone is the sorrow, gone doubt and fear,
For you love me truly, truly dear."

The lyrics seemed so appropriate and resonated so personally for us, given everything we had overcome to be with one another. After the concert we went to *The Tremont Hotel* where a special Valentine's Day dinner was served.

Galveston: 1900 A Storm, A Story of Twin Flames
CHAPTER 23

Genevieve's Diary: The Holiday

The Tremont

24th December 1899

Yesterday I finished wrapping the gifts that I made for my beloved Uri. From fine wool yarn I knit two pairs of mittens to keep his hands warm on these very cold winter days. I also wrapped six silk handkerchiefs on which I embroidered his initials, U.P., in script style.

Uri and I had such a joyful time a number of weeks ago when I helped him decorate his Christmas tree. After that we hung many balls of mistletoe from the ceiling. Of course I had to kiss him after each of the mistletoes was hung.

Tonight my sweet Uri will meet us (Mother and Father included) for midnight Mass. Tomorrow we spend our very first Christmas together! Peter and Karina have invited us to their house for Christmas dinner, and I still have to bake the plum pudding and prepare the wassail bowl. So it be best I hurry.

2nd January 1900

A New Year and a New Century! I can't wait, for April 18 when I marry my beloved. We had such a grand time last night at "The Olympia" with so much dancing, a great dinner, and "the grandest display of fireworks Galveston has ever seen." 1.900 fireworks ignited at midnight. As soon as the fireworks ceased Uri held me in his arms and all there in the glow of candlelight sang "To Auld Lang Syne."

14th February 1900

A few minutes ago I heard a knock on the door and answered it to find a man delivering two-dozen red roses and a large heart shaped box of chocolates. My dear Uri, he is so sweet. He thinks of everything. He told me that he has made something especially for me, which he will bring when he comes for me later. We will be celebrating Valentine Day by attending a concert at Harmony Hall. From there we will have dinner at The Tremont.

I plan to wear the beautiful dress Uri gave me for Christmas. The white with red accents make the outfit just perfect for Valentines.

I have a cake baking in the oven made with all my love and shaped like a heart. I can't wait to see him!

1st March 1900

We have been so busy making preparations, and I can't wait to be with my Uri. Husband and wife alas.

Uri had classes yesterday and I picked him up in front of St. Mary's School. He has been so dedicated to his conversion classes, and I know it's all for me.

"Hello, my love." He said as he climbed into the buggy.

"How was class today?"

"Actually, quite boring." He smiled jokingly.

"I'd much rather be studying my Chemistry book, but if this is what it takes to marry you, I guess I'll have to do it."

"Where to now?"

"Peter and Karina have invited us to dinner."

He took the reins and with a snap we were off to his brother's for dinner.

Galveston: 1900 A Storm, A Story of Twin Flames

CHAPTER 24

The Wedding

St. Mary's Church

Our wedding day had finally arrived: April 18, 1900. All preparations had been made with no detail left to chance. I wanted it to be absolutely perfect for my Princess. With Genevieve's help in designing the invitations, I printed one hundred and twenty cards. The print on the card was surrounded by a pattern of lace with a cherub on either side of this lace motif. For the letters themselves, I used black ink along with gold leaf.

The wedding celebration was to be held at the *Garten Verein* located at N. Street and 27th. The *Garten* consisted of a social pavilion where parties and gatherings were held as well as its surrounding park with its tailored landscape, fountain, and statues. Catering was to provided by the chiefs at *The Tremont Hotel*, and the meal was to consist of fresh tossed salad, Russian caviar, New York Strip, carrots and mashed potatoes. As for drinks, we would serve wine, vodka, and champagne.

The large wedding cake would stand on a latticed base. The edges of the cake were to be decorated with weaved lines of frosting that undulated up and down. The sides of the cake would have sunflowers made of frosting. On the top, there would be a small vase shaped like a cupola from which delicate flowers would be placed.

Three sets of String Quartets would play. One would play inside the pavilion and the other two would be outside in the park, with one Quartet by the fountain and the other by the statue that stood before *Ursuline Academy*. After dinner, a band would provide music for dancing. Photos were to be taken by *The Strand Photography Company*, using the latest camera by Eastman Kodak. The Strand Photography would even take photos after darkness fell by using *blitzlicht*, the newly developed flash powder.

For transportation, I had commissioned an enclosed carriage pulled by a set of four white horses that would pick up Genevieve, along with her parents, and take them to the Church where I would await her.

The night before was sleepless for me in my state of anticipation. I arose at dawn and dressed in my tailcoat suit, top hat and white gloves. Peter picked me up in his carriage, and we were on our way to *St. Mary's Church*, a short ride from my Villa.

The Church was shaped in the form of a Cross and had a turret topped with a metal cone on either side of the front. We entered the keyhole shaped door and stepped into coolness of the interior. Behind the altar was a massive stained glass window of Jesus and the Disciples. To the right of the altar was an impressive organ.

Soon the guests began filing in. From the back of the Church where I had stationed myself, I greeted them as I saw them enter. Shortly thereafter, Karina and the children were milling about the Church. From my vantage point in the back, I then saw Karina walk up to the front of the Church and say something to the Priest who was making preparations there at the altar. Among those who entered and wished me well were Mrs. Hopkins who escorted her four children, Dr. and Mrs. Young, Isaac and Cora Cline, and Isaac's brother Joseph.

Justus and Michael, each accompanied by his wife, also made their way into the Church. When Genevieve's Father and Mother entered I checked my pocket watch and noted that the start was imminent. Accompanying her parents were both sets of grandparents, one from San Antonio and the other from Fort Worth. My thoughts briefly turned to my own parents, so far away in Russia. The letter they had sent wishing Genevieve and me the best, along with their love and blessings comforted me. The Church was now full and buzzing with anticipation and excitement.

The organist then sat at his bench and began playing. I quickly took my place at the altar and looked back. As the organist commenced playing Mendelssohn's *"Wedding March"*, a figure emerged from the shadows and into the rays of light that were pouring from the top windows situated at the front of the Church. There she was, standing next to her Father. She wore a breathtaking Edwardian wedding dress with fine chiffon and guipure lace. Her dress was laced at the shoulders and laced flowers ran across her waist. She wore long white sleeves that ended in white-gloved hands. She held in those wonderful hands, a bouquet of deep red roses.

Her dress flowed straight down her body and ended in fine ruffled silk. Her hair was gathered on top, pompadour style, and on top of her hair she wore a puffy laced headdress that ran the back of her head. Every eye was fixed on her, a true Princess on her wedding day. I gathered in my breath, as I seemed to have stopped inhaling.

Her Father escorted her to the altar, and there in front of perhaps one hundred and seventy five people we were married.

Galveston: 1900 A Storm, A Story of Twin Flames

CHAPTER 25

Celebration at the Garten Verein

Garten Verein

After the ceremony, we exited the Church and were greeted by the enclosed carriage drawn by the four white horses, waiting for us on the street in front of the Church. The carriage driver upon seeing us opened the door, and we climbed into the plush white velvet interior. The driver then closed the door and climbed up to the perch where he shook the reins. With the happy sound of clopping hoofs, the carriage made its way West on Broadway and down Bath Avenue to N. Street.

Upon arriving, I helped Genevieve out of the carriage. We heard music wafting from the *Garten Verein*. The String Quartet had started. On the near side of the *Garten* was the pavilion, a large octagonal, two-story building with verandas surrounding the lower level. The upper level had circular windows and a slanted roof with a small cupola on top. I glanced around and smiled. The *Garten* was a lovely sight with its large oak trees, short palms, carefully selected shrubs and flowers. It provided a reprieve for quiet contemplation and for connection with nature, all in the middle of the bustling city.

At the head table we sat with Peter, Karina, their children as well as Genevieve's parents. As soon as all the guests assembled the first thing that we did was cut the wedding cake, as was the custom in those days. While French Hors d'oeuvres, including *basil plamiers*, and *crudités*, were being served, Genevieve, myself and our family headed out into the park along with the photographer.

We first assembled in front of the sizable, metallic fountain located at the far end of the park where the photographer took pictures. The fountain had an octagonal base with a twenty-foot column from which water splashed onto three successively larger pans. It made a fine backdrop for our pictures. During this process, we had an audience as many guests had gathered in this area to listen to one of the String Quartets that played just to one side.

After posing and photographing varying combinations of family members in front of the fountain, the photographer then directed us to a new location and posed Genevieve and me, followed by more combinations of family members in front of one of the Renaissance styled, marble statues that decorated the grounds.

We then retuned to the octagonal dining hall where all the champagne glasses had been filled and dinner was in the process of being served. Peter interrupted the noisy chatter by striking a fork against his champagne glass.

"*Pozdravlyayu.* Congratulations, Let's drink to love, *Gorka!*" He said raising his glass of champagne toward Genevieve and me.

"May God grant you a life filled with health, happiness, and peace."

He added to the cheers of our guests.

As what is the Russian tradition, Peter then offered us bread and salt, which we both partook. Genevieve's Father then followed with a toast of his own.

During dinner, a Russian dance troupe provided a rousing performance that was very much enjoyed by all.

The rest of the evening was filled with music, dancing, and laughter. We particularly enjoyed the first dance of the evening, which Genevieve and I had selected, the waltz, *"After the Ball"*. All eyes were on my beautiful Princess, in all her magnificence, as we swayed around the dance floor. This dance was followed by another waltz, *"And the Band Played On"*, which we were joined on the dance floor by members of our family. After much more dancing by everyone in attendance, it was time for us to leave and as was the custom in those days, for good luck, Genevieve retied the laces of her shoes before leaving the pavilion.

As we exited the building, our family and guests followed us to the horse drawn carriage, its side lanterns now lit. As we climbed in, our guests commenced throwing rice at us. The carriage driver immediately closed the door behind us and ascended to the perch. With the patter of grains of rice hitting the window, the pop of the flash powder, and the resultant strobe illuminating the night, it seemed as though a small thundershower was rumbling in the far distance. As the carriage now moved forward, we heard the muffled shouts and cheers from our well-wishers slowly fading off into the distance. Immersed in each other's eyes, oblivious to everything happening outside, we kissed.

Galveston: 1900 A Storm, A Story of Twin Flames

CHAPTER 26

Alone At Last

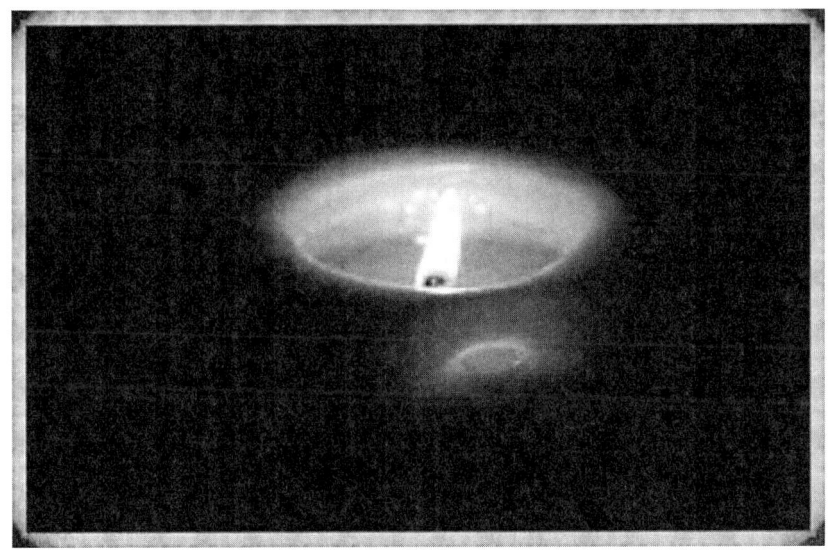

After sharing many kisses with Genevieve along the way, we arrived home and the carriage driver swung open the carriage door and wished us a good night before riding off. We walked up the doorsteps to the Villa. I opened the door and carried her in my arms, up the steps and into our bedroom. The room was completely aglow with soft candlelight, as I had made arrangements beforehand to surprise her. I carefully placed her on the bed.

"How lovely. You always think of everything."

Her eyes were alight with the glow of candlelight and filled with absolute happiness.

"Thank you for making me so happy." I whispered softly into her ear.

Her perfume, *"Fougere Royale"*, wafted softly from her neck, and filled my senses.

I slowly began undressing her: first removing the veil from her hair and then her dress, and as I did so she unbutton my shirt helping me slip out of it. We undressed totally, nothing hidden from the other, in full honesty.

And there she was, illuminated by the gentle glow of candlelight, her body so magnificent with only the heart locket hanging between her breasts. I moved forward and kissed her, caressing the curve of her breasts, moving down to the curve of her hips. We kissed till our lips were numb. A thousand kisses like an endless strand of lovely pearls on a necklace. I moved on top of her, our bodies intertwined. Even now I can still feel her firm nipples on my chest. I can still hear her reverberations echo in my mind as our bodies united.

Now she slowly moved on top of me. Her body and breasts gently swaying. I could see the heart locket, interspersed between us, but connected to our resplendent heartbeats, undulating with glints of candlelight catching its golden surface.

We died in each other's arms that night. And aroused within the Soul of the Universe. Each second of that night was an encounter with the Divine and with eternity. It was a union of body that replenished the supernal soul. It was a realm of purity and perfection. It was as if our lovemaking was helping heal the Universal Soul.

In this realm of unmitigated truth, there was no hatred, no family strife, and no desecration of Nature, only splendid consonance.

It was, a realm of perfect harmonic resonance, and pure Oneness. It was a night of preeminent bliss. At night that never was... A night that will never be again. Much later we fell asleep wrapped in each others arms, our very redolence becoming one, the trace of musty sweetness

Galveston: 1900 A Storm, A Story of Twin Flames

clinging to the morning dew, clothed only in a placid veil of delicate fatigue and complete fulfillment.

Galveston: 1900 A Storm, A Story of Twin Flames

CHAPTER 27

New Orleans

Oak Alley

For our honeymoon, we were to travel to New Orleans, Louisiana via the *Mallory Line Steamship Company*. With the help of Peter, we had unloaded all our trunks on Pier 24 and stood waiting, along with a multitude of other passengers, to embark onto the **S.S. Lampasas**, a single funneled coal liner. Soon we were on our way, sailing east on the Gulf.

The trip would take only a day. I had previously taken this same Line all the way to New York City a number of years earlier. That journey, with all its stops, took more than fourteen days.

> *As arduous as the voyage to New York was, it paled in comparison to what Peter and I went through on our trip from Russia to Texas. We left our little village of Shlisselburg; a village founded by Peter the Great in 1702. In May 1894, It was heartbreaking to leave Mother, and I remember how she cried when Peter and I first presented my idea to move to the New World, but with time she came to accept it for she knew that our chances of finding a good life were much better there. Peter and I saved for our journey for over three years. Peter earned extra money, when not helping Father, by working at a print shop in St. Petersburg, and I managed to save money by working extra hours as a field hand at the neighbor's farm.*
>
> *I had dreamed of a different life since I was a child and had reoccurring dreams, ever since I could remember, of living in a place of sand and surf. And of something else... Something more profound, something involving fulfilling the essence of my very being. The latter was more of a feeling...a sense of perfected actuality and culmination. This dream motif and feeling, which I experienced in many forms, never left me and just increased until the very day I arrived in Galveston.*
>
> *Shlisselburg had as its main landmark Oreshek Fortress, a sprawling fort complex completely walled with numerous towers; some round and others square, interspersed throughout the perimeter. Oreshek sits on an island in Lake Ladoga at the head of the River Neva.*
>
> *The area was also known for Old Ladoga Canal, a project of Peter the Great that formed a water transportation route, one of the first of its kind in Russia, linking the Neva to the Sivir River. Under the poverty of the serf style system, we*

all (Father, Peter, our oldest sibling Pavel, and me) toiled, working the soil to bring forth the very nourishment that kept us alive. We grew rye and oats and also attended to a few farm animals: a cow, some chickens, and some pigs.

So we left in May just as the weather started warming and the sun was just starting to thaw the permafrost that now had yielded to spouts of green. While I only took one trunk, Peter and Karina had a total of four, having to pack for my then two-year-old niece Shasha, and my one-year-old nephew Sergei. Included in my truck was my prized Chess book by Isya Shumov, which helped me master the game and win some matches held in St. Petersburg. Also packed in my trunk were my treasured scarves Mother had knitted for me over the years. Father, Peter and I loaded our trunks onto the cart, the bright sunshine poring into the cool brisk air.

The flat land upon which sat our country village was filled with large deciduous trees that were just budding their fist spring foliage. While Father and I rode in one cart with the trunks and luggage, Mother, Peter, Karina, and the children rode in the other cart. By the time we reached the train station in St. Petersburg our buttocks were quite sore from the bumps and ditches we traversed as we rode over the rough, jarring dirt roads.

At the train station, we exchanged painful goodbyes and boarded the train. I sat by the window, the train whistling its last blast, as I watched tears flow down Mother's face. I felt a massive lump form in my throat, and I did my utmost to hold my own tears back. As the train crept forward she hurled kisses out to us with her hand. My heart sank with sorrow at leaving Mother, but certain at the same time that Peter and I were doing the right thing, and that we were finding our rightful place in the Universe.

A ten-day trip led us to the port of Marseille on the French Coast. Along the way, we rode through Austria-Hungary where the sight of the majestic Alps capped in pure white snow left us mesmerized. Never before had I seen such imposing natural wonders. From Austria-Hungary we crossed the German Empire and entered the Black Forrest, so appropriately named, as the sun began its descent into the western horizon. My mind now drifted back to the past.

I recalled how much talk of Revolution pervaded the last three years of my life in Russia. It all seemed so distant now, an almost forgotten memory like the thick dark that was now engulfing the massive fir trees whirring pass the train window before me, The next morning we were well into the French Republic where we passed though countless fields and vineyards.

    At Marseille, we boarded the **S.S. La Bourgogne** to embark on our 8-day trip to New York. Before boarding, along with the multitude of other steerage passengers, we filed past the Medical Officer who inspected us for disease.

    On board the single men (as well as women) were directed to cabins where up to six to a bunk were quartered. Peter, Karina and the children fared much better in a tiny yet private cabin afforded to families. The food was plain yet tolerable.

    The Purser did his best to ensure that attendants made our trip as tolerable as possible. Unfortunately, an outbreak of a stomach virus and traversing some rough waters brought about by inclement weather somewhere in the North Atlantic, left chamber pots overflowing and the stench of vomit heavy in the air.

    It was midday when we finally arrived in New York harbor where a dizzying array of buildings spewed out from Manhattan Island. So massive were the number and size of the edifices that it seemed to me to be just a matter of time before the Island would slip into the inky, dark waters of the harbor below. Just opposite the City, we passed the Statue of Liberty perched upon Bedloe's Island, her upright hand holding a torch, a beacon of hope to the "tired, poor, huddled masses yearning to breathe free." Those very words seemed to be written expressly for us who were crammed in steerage. After a brief stay, allowing for those arriving at their destination to disembark and others to board, we were again on our way sailing south around Florida and into the Gulf of Mexico.

    I was virtually sleepless with anticipation the night before arriving in Galveston. I arose before dawn, quietly made my way to the upper deck where I was greeted by the warm humid air of the Texas Gulf. How different this was compared to cold, frigid Russia, yet even as out of my element I seemed to be, without hardly knowing any English, never was I more sure in my certitude that this was my destiny.

    I looked above and could see the smoke from the two, hissing funnels blending seamlessly into the foggy air. Gazing east I could now just make out the first glow of rays emerging from the black expanse at the horizon. The ship plowed onward, its wake clearly visible in the ocean water below me. Looking around, I now saw that I was not alone having been joined on deck by a handful of other early risers.

    A short time later, I saw it for the very first time: a jeweled city shrouded in a veil of fog, like an image from a nether world, hovering just above the level of the sea. I could see the light of the early morn sun sifting through the cupolas and steeples of this enchanting city, setting them aglow. I could see the trestle that stretched over the Gulf at the city's midpoint, its supporting beams encased in the water's foamy splendor.

    It was a much smaller version of New York but far more quaint and charming. I felt a vague sense of déjà vu that emanated from the recesses of my subconscious, as though perhaps the familiarity that lay before me was from a scene from one of my reoccurring dreams.

    Seeing this City for the first time, alight on an island of golden sand, the dawn's radiant sunshine reflecting on azure, lapping waves, like hands enveloping the City's perimeter, secured my conviction, to the very core, that this was my rightful place in the Universe. That this was the only place I could find true happiness. For this was the very place, the only place, I would find her.

    The **Lampasas** was quite a marvel, and in fact, it was advertised as a "floating hotel." By our experience, it certainly lived up to that reputation. That evening in the dining hall, we were served a delightful five-course meal. After dinner, we retired to the lounge for some of our favorite champagne, exquisite *Veuve Clicquot Ponsardin*. The lounge was a mahogany-paneled room lined with many curtain draped, ocean-facing rectangular windows, as well as leather couches and chairs.

    We made beautiful love that night our bodies undulating to the slight roll of the ship. The morning after breakfast, we took a stroll on the deck. We then stopped by the guardrail, and while Genevieve peered off into the distance, I just beheld her: the breeze wildly swirling her hair about her face. The umber rays of morning sunlight were reflecting from the surface of the water and onto her face and onto her wavy hair. She looked like a woman right out of the pages of *Vogue Magazine*. Sensing my eyes on her, she then turned to face me, smiled, and leaned forward to give me a kiss.

Disembarking at New Orleans, we stayed at a fine hotel in the French Quarter near Jackson Square. For the first time, we tried Cajun Cuisine, a spicy local taste particular to that region of the Country. Dishes such as Gumbo Creole, Jambalaya, and Etouffee, although new to our palate, were thoroughly delicious. New Orleans also offered much in the way of entertaining plays. We attended a few of them including **Ben Hur**, **Sherlock Holmes**, and **Cyrano DeBergerac**.

From New Orleans were took the mid-sized riverboat, *Irene*, propelled by its massive rear paddle wheel, and traveling west on the Mississippi toward Baton Rouge, headed to antebellum Oak Alley Plantation. On the way there, the views from *"Old Man River"* as the locals called the Mississippi were fabulous. Towering green trees, oaks with hanging Spanish moss, flowering magnolias, filled the view as far as the eye could see.

Some of the scenery also included, bayous and swamps where we saw alligators absorbing late springtime sun on the banks of the water. Birds of every type were everywhere, flying across the skies overhead, crossing in the distance in front of the riverboat, and migrating within the canopy of the forests. I reflected on how different, green Louisiana was as compared to sandy, salty-aired Galveston.

At *Oak Alley Plantation*, the riverboat stopped, and from the banks of the Mississippi, we could see its immense two-story Greek revival mansion, perhaps two hundred yards away, framed by double rowed, colossal oaks. These giants, like a row of sentries, formed a canopied path that led from the river to the front steps of the mansion. Off to the side and away from the mansion were small ramshackle dwellings that housed the sharecroppers. While one of the porters recounted the history of the plantation, all of us passengers enjoyed a picnic, served by the riverboat attendants, there on the banks, beneath the branches of a towering oak.

Galveston: 1900 A Storm, A Story of Twin Flames

CHAPTER 28

Journey Back Home

The S.S. Lampasas

On the way back to Galveston, we again traveled on the ***Lampasas***. Early that evening, we retired to our plush cabin and fell asleep. Soon thereafter we awakened, stirred by a sudden rolling of the ship.

"Uri, what's happening?" Genevieve uttered with concern.

I got out of bed and peered out the window of our cabin. A flash of lighting lit up the skies, reflecting on sizable waves.

"We've run into a storm."

I climbed back into bed and cradled her in my arms.

"I hate storms…." She whispered.

As we embraced each other, I kissed her forehead as a sign of reassurance. Fortunately, the squall passed within a short twenty minutes, and soon we were back in the land of dreams.

CHAPTER 29

An Evening with Friends

Once home again, Genevieve at her own insistence took charge of most of the duties of the house. Some of Mary's services were still retained such as helping clean the house and helping Genevieve prepare dinner when guests were invited for the evening. As far as the Orphanage was concerned, Genevieve resigned from her job, but continued volunteering on Saturdays, as she still wished to see the children.

During a particular fall evening, I recall we had invited Justus and Michael along with their respective wives for dinner. After the meal, Genevieve, who had learned piano as a child while in the Church choir, retired with our female guests to the music room where she entertained them by playing the piano. I had recently purchased this piano for her after we had returned from New Orleans.

While the ladies were in the music room, Justus, Michael and me made our way to the parlor where I lit a pipe, and they each enjoyed a cigar. We then engaged in a lively discussion of the current state of Medicine. We recounted some of the recent discoveries that we were aware of such as Ronald Ross' deduction that malaria was transmitted by the bite of the *anopheles mosquito*, and that rat fleas were the mode of transmission for the Bubonic plague. Justus related to us that his Druggist Store was now carrying aspirin, a new drug by the German chemist, Felix Hoffman. This miracle medicine reduced pain, inflammation, and fever.

Although these advances were very exciting, we also seemed to agree that on the pharmaceutical side of things, we still had a long way to go. "Snake Oil" was readily sold by quacks, by mail order, and falsely promised to cure ailments ranging from cancer to gastritis.

Another category of drugs, Cordials, were readily available and were touted by many for general well being. They usually contained some cocaine as an active ingredient. Cough cordials contained, as an active ingredient, some heroin. We noted that the scientific community was beginning to raise concerns regarding the side effects of these agents, as they seemed to possess addictive properties. Michael then pointed out that Coca Cola, the beverage, had as one its secret ingredients; coca leafs which also contained small amounts of cocaine.

I smiled as I looked at Justus and asserted. "It must be one of your best sellers at the Drug Store."

"Perhaps, I can't seem to keep it on the shelf." He countered smugly.

We ended with a discussion on lunacy, and all agreed that treatment for mental disease was basically nonexistent at this time. With that, we each partook of a nightcap of whiskey ant then joined our ladies in the music room.

Galveston: 1900 A Storm, A Story of Twin Flames

CHAPTER 30

Frozen

The Blizzard of 26th November 1898, Galveston Bay

The new century brought with it a devastating blizzard that swept most of the Nation including Galveston. Reaching the City with wind gusts up to eighty miles per hour, the temperature dropped to eight degrees and piles of snow accumulated everywhere including the beach.

Genevieve and I hunkered down at home with every single chimney and even the stove lit. Trying to keep from freezing, we even walked around the house with blankets wrapped around us.

After a few days it warmed up enough to venture out into a temperature of 30 degrees. I had received a call from Peter the day before, and we agreed to meet at our Shop so that we could make progress on now delayed work. As I approached the Shop, Peter was already waiting outside.

"Yeye chertovski kholodno (It's damn cold.)" I declared.

Half smiling, he replied. *"Daje yvagaushiv gebia hozain ne osfault sobaku na vlize vfakoy holod. (It's so cold that the good owner would not let his dog out.) I want to show you something. Follow me."*

While we walked the short distance to the Wharf, plumes of white condensation from our breath attacked the path ahead of us. Peter filled me in on the details from the newspaper accounts he had read.

"The cold snap was so severe that icebergs were reported floating down the Mississippi, at New Orleans. I even read that Niagara Falls was frozen over." He reported with a trace of astonishment in his voice.

"Oh boy…" I muttered.

The blizzard had transformed the landscape, enveloping the entire city in a cold gray, icy veil. Everything around us seemed absolutely motionless, as if held in a state of suspended animation. Hearing only the tapping of our shoes on the sidewalk, we walked past the massive red-bricked *Texas Star Flour Mills* factory that turned east Texas wheat into flour. We now plodded under the ramp that led from the upper floors of the factory to the pier where the product would be loaded onto ships. Arriving at the Bay, I saw a world transformed. Between the fifteen-storied coal elevator at Pier 34 and the equally tall grain elevator at Pier 14, I saw many vessels, including the shrimp boats, sailing ships, and some large steamers, adjacent to the docks, but resting at an oddly lower levels. The Bay itself also looked very peculiar and… unfamiliar.

My mind was racing to figure out what had happened when it hit me. Most of the water from the Bay was now gone! In its wake, vast areas of expansive mud flats and immense islands of gray green occupied what was once water. Moving out over the pier, I looked closely at one of these green colored islands. I then realized they were exposed sea grass that grew at the bottom of the Bay.

"The wind blew the water from the Bay over the Island and into the Gulf." Peter said answering the question in my mind.

I now concentrated on a dark fringe of gray blue, lining the Bay edge as far as my eye could see. A closer view allowed me to realize that this fringe was comprised of a pile of fish, interspersed with shrimp, four foot wide and one foot thick.

"My God, look at all those fish!" I said incredulously.

"Absolutely, unbelievable." Peter stuttered through frozen teeth.

We were now really getting cold, our feet burning from the artic air.

"Let's get back to the Shop." Peter asserted.

With that we turned around and retraced our steps back to the Strand.

Galveston: 1900 A Storm, A Story of Twin Flames

CHAPTER 31

Calm Before The Storm

**Dining Three Stories Above The Waves at *The Bon Ton*
(*Pagoda Bath House* Visible to The Right)**

Courtesy of The Galveston Historical Foundation

The spring before my whole world changed was idyllic filled with laughter, fun, and romantic love. One of my favorite rituals was to surprise Genevieve by casually leaving a rose or wrapped candy somewhere in the house where she would eventually come across it while I was at work.

During this time Genevieve spent some time reading and completed Stoker's **Dracula** and Wells' **War of the Worlds**, sharing the plot with me as she read them. Together we worked to fill our solarium with beautiful ferns and flowering plants.

During the later part of May, I accepted an invitation by Michael to hunt quail in the coastal prairie region just south of Houston. I was a pretty decent shot, as Peter and I were taught to bird hunt back in Russia when we were young.

Michael and I left Galveston on the Santa Fe Railroad, crossing the Bay over the three-mile wooden trestle, the steam locomotive that pulled our Pullman spewing a thick layer of ash into the atmosphere above. While crossing the Bay by train, one had the illusion of floating above the surface of the water, as there were no guardrails that would give the perspective of traveling over a bridge. To our right ran the two other train trestles and to our left was the wooden wagon bridge.

Looking out the train window at the wagon bridge, I saw numerous horse drawn buggies and wagons crossing in both directions. On this particular day, I beheld that the angle of the sun caused the whitecaps of the Bay to reflect into a thousand brilliant points of almost blinding light.

The edge of the Bay was lined with lush marshes, tall grass prairie, pampas, and beyond the border of the water with sparse clusters of oak. As we crossed over to the Texas mainland, I sighed as my thoughts turned to Genevieve and how I already missed her. Fortunately, the hunting trip was short and I was back home within two days.

For my birthday, Genevieve surprised me with tickets to the Grand Opera where we saw *"Sadko"* by the Great Russian composer Nikolai Rimsky-Kosakov. That evening, my princess looked so stunning, her hair drawn up into a waterfall of curls. She wore the long satin red dress that flared at the bottom with red velvet accents that I had bought for her in New Orleans. Walking about the theater, she turned many heads. She was the consummate "Gibson Girl", tall and slender, gorgeous, full of calm confidence.

"Sadko" featured a beautiful song, *"The Viking Trades Song"* whose notes filled me with nostalgia. I thought of my parents and how I wanted to share my Genevieve with them, especially Mother. I found

solace in the fact that Genevieve and I planned to visit them the next summer. The trip to St. Petersburg would be quite an ordeal. Ten days for the transatlantic trip to France and then another six days by train to St. Petersburg.

When we returned home, Genevieve surprised me with a German Chocolate birthday cake she had made and placed in the parlor. That enchanted night ended with passionate, tender lovemaking on the chair, then on the parlor couch, and finally on the plush Oriental rug. Lovemaking that was always pristine and absolutely uninhibited. From where I was situated from behind, I collapsed next to her, embracing her, both of us in a heap of fatigued felicity, covered with a thick layer of perspiration that belied the brisk early morning air.

With the heat that the late spring brought, we spent time on the beach where we would swim and picnic. We would often lunch at *"Bon Ton on the Sea."* the roof top café at *Murdoch's Bath House*. *Ton* translated and referred to the upper 10,000 relating to the wealthy upper class circles of New York society and by extension to other metropolitan areas. *Bon Ton,* therefore meant the good (high) society, and how appropriate a name for the restaurant three stories atop the waves.

The featured specialties of *Bon Ton* were fish chowder, chili, and *Khahn's Ice Cream* for dessert, all served on fine crystal, on top of tables covered with white cloth, and fine silverware. As far as the chili, spicy beef mixed with pinto beans, was concerned, I must admit that it took a few tries before it became one of my favorites. The Russian man had finally succumbed to real Texan food.

Our usual dining spot was on the Gulf side where the soothing sea breeze blew off a carpet of water as far as the eye could see. Just to our right stood *Pagoda*, the very spot where we had shared our very first real conversation. Hovering above the surf, both Bathhouses were like long, giant steamships suspended in frozen animation above the churning of the water below.

Our conversations were sublime, without boundaries and no topic off limits. I can still hear my Genevieve giggling at some of my silly remarks, throwing her head slightly back, and flashing that most impeccable smile in the most captivating, sensual way that was uniquely hers. Our words flowing like a masterful symphony, ebbing and flowing with the humming of the vibration of the waves below, discussing anything and everything that came to mind. From the most profound to the frivolous did it flow from thought to thought, to hopes and to dreams. Such was the depth of her beautiful mind.

As far as Peter was concerned, he had tremendous success in growing our business by hiring a number of "drummers". This was the term for salesman at that time because they drummed up business. These drummers traveled to the nearby towns of Baytown, Texas City, and La Porte where they peddled our printing services, with much success. That was my brother, the natural born businessman.

Galveston: 1900 A Storm, A Story of Twin Flames

CHAPTER 32

Louise Hopkins, Dr. Samuel Young and Isaac Cline

Samuel & Jenny Young

The Levy Building

The Levy Building

The magnitude of how many were lost on that cursed day now once again hit me, perhaps as many as 12,000. Too many to count.

Years later after the *1905 Rosenburg Library*, the oldest continually running library in Texas, was built, residents chronicled the tragedy by gathering photos and memoirs and storing them there in a permanent collection. I recall reading some of those accounts in **"The Galveston News"**. Louise Hopkins, whose mother was a friend of the Parker family, wrote one such memoir. Louise lived with her widowed mother and two brothers, John and Mason, and sister Lois in a long rectangular bungalow near *Old Red* and *Sealy Hospital* on the eastern Bay side of the Island.

After her Father's death, her Mother added a second floor to the residence in which rooms were available for rent. These rooms were mostly occupied by Medical Students and allowed her Mother to earn an income without leaving the children.

Louise remembered playing in her yard with her seven year old friend Martha that morning, the rain soaking and muddying their dresses. When the rain fell particularly hard they would run to the porch laughing. It was "a children's paradise". Soon the street looked like a brown river. They witnessed pieces of wood, small tree limbs, trinkets, thousands of toads, and even a snake flowing through the water swollen street in front of their houses.

Later, still in the early afternoon, the children spotted even more items in the flowing current, including a child's toy. This toy frightened them, and they each retreated into their respective home.

Once inside, the family began to transfer cooking supplies, *"Tidal Wave Flour"*, sacks of coffee and sugar to the second floor. Her Maltese kitten was very skittish and kept following her around the house. After moving the supplies to safer ground, Mrs. Hopkins located an ax stored in a closet and without warning began chopping holes in the floor. The children could only watch in stunned silence. Water immediately began to rush into the house through these holes and cover the fine wooden floor that comprised the lower level. Mrs. Hopkins took this action in order to help anchor the house, a measure that was repeated by many residents throughout the city.

The entire family then gathered in one of the rooms upstairs where Mrs. Hopkins had placed a drum of lard with a wick in the center of the room, lit it, and thus created a makeshift candle. The winds, now tremendous, threatened to tear the eastern wall of the house from its junction at the ceiling. Terrorized, the family made plans to use mattresses as floatation devises in the event the house collapsed into the sea that now covered the Island.

After the storm finally passed, the Hopkins family stepped outside to survey their uninsured, devastated home: The two upstairs bedrooms, and the downstairs dining room and kitchen had been blown into the yard next door. Their livelihood and home had been ruined, but they were grateful to be alive.

Dr. Samuel Young, my client and amateur weather enthusiast, also wrote an extensive, account of the day's events. He recounts that at dawn September 8th he rode to the beach in order to observe the sky and its implications for the weather. At the Midway, he encountered Isaac Cline who was making his own weather observations. There, standing on the beach, both men watched the streetcar trestle that stretched over the water attacked by large phosphorescent waves. Waves that exploded into vertical geysers as they hit the wood columns supporting the trestle. The winds were blowing from the North, but oddly the waves of the Gulf were actually running against the wind direction.

Dr. Young then asked Isaac what the latter made of what they were seeing. Isaac said that it looked as though a storm was headed toward the city. He tried to reassure Dr. Young that the latter should not worry, given that the Weather Bureau, the entity that issued forecasts for the Nation from its headquarters in Washington D.C. using data gathered at field offices such as the one in Galveston, had not issued any storm warnings. Young disagreed and told Isaac that to him it looked like something big was incoming. Dr. Young then hurriedly went to the Western Union Telegraph Station located on the Strand and composed a message that was sent to his wife who was in San Antonio. His wife was scheduled to return by train later that day, but Dr. Young urged her to remain where she was as "a large storm was upon them."

Dr. Young then rode back to his house at Bath Ave. and P Street, located less than four blocks from the Gulf where he busily secured the all windows and doors. Once he finished and as the fury of the tempest had truly began, he looked out of a second floor window from which he saw cisterns, barrels, small shacks, and even an outhouse floating down the street through the water.

In the late evening, as the full fury of the Storm was striking, Dr. Young, who now had moved upstairs, heard a loud thumping emanating from the downstairs. Lighting a candle he proceeded halfway down the stairs and realized that the seawater had risen to nearly the level of the entire first floor. The noise he was hearing was from the downstairs furniture bumping against the ceiling.

Now amidst the booming claps of thunder and the deafening howl of the wind, Dr. Young decided to open the door that led to the second floor gallery so that he could see what was happening outside. As he opened it, he was immediately blown back into the hallway. He was absolutely amazed by the Storm's intensity and fought his way back to the doorway by inching his way along the wall and used doorknobs to pull himself forward. He grabbed the doorframe and heaved himself through the doorway and onto the porch. His jaw dropped as he witnessed the unbelievable scene: What he saw was akin to what one sees while being on a ship. Immense waves with large pieces of wreckage were sweeping through his neighborhood.

The only house that remained standing began to slowly turn, and then rise, before sailing off into the night. The colossal winds then pinned him to the edge of the doorway. The water now climbed to the level of the second floor, and the structural integrity of the house started to falter. As one of the gallery's supporting beams tore loose it struck Dr. Young on the head leaving him bloodied and dazed. He now turned his head and saw that the force of the rain striking the house was so great that the drops were exploding into the wall as tiny sparkles of light.

As he realized that the entire house was about to collapse, he grabbed the door leading to the porch and mounted it. Almost immediately the structure crumbled beneath him. Using the door as a raft, he kicked as hard as he could to put distance between himself and the pile of tangled wood that was once his house. The motion of the current from the tidal surge then propelled him North past the *Garten Verein* and then Northwest. With the wind surging over his body and freezing rain striking him like porcupine needles, his raft finally docked against a mound of rubble upon which he remained for the next eight hours.

Isaac Cline's account was even more dramatic and heartbreaking. His brother, Joseph Cline, an assistant at the Galveston Weather Bureau, wrote the memoir. At 2:00 p.m. the day of The Storm, Isaac was on the third floor of the Levy Building, where he had been recording barometric pressure as well as noting wind speed from an anemometer that had been mounted on the top floor of the building. Joseph was busy answering the phone as worried, frantic residents reported on damages caused by the sudden turn in bad weather.

With the winds reaching gale force, Isaac looked out the window facing the Bay side of the Island and saw that water from the Bay had been pushed over the Wharf and onto the city streets. Moving to the windows on the other side, he saw that seawater from the Gulf had also spilled over the streets on that side of the Island. From what he just had seen, it appeared as though the entire Island was sinking.

Isaac then composed an urgent cable to Willis Moore, the Chief of the Weather Bureau in Washington D. C., in which he reported that the city was going under water fast, and he feared that many lives would be lost. He urged Moore to send help. He next handed the message to Joseph who hurried to take it to the telegraph office. Through driving rain, Isaac made his way home located at Bath Ave and Q Street, a few blocks from the Gulf, through knee-deep water and finally arrived there around 3:30 p.m. By the time Joseph arrived, a couple of hours later, at least fifty neighbors had sought refuge within the well-constructed, sturdy Cline house.

Joseph tried to convince Isaac and the others to go back to the center of the City, but Isaac was resolute to stay. He insisted that his pregnant wife Cora was in no condition to be moved. Isaac now checked on the progress of the Storm by looking outside the front door and was astonished by the transformation of the neighborhood. The entire scene was of open water that was interrupted by only a few recognizable structures such as the second floor of homes, and telegraph poles. The sea then rose four feet in four seconds, and poured through the doorway.

Everyone who was downstairs now scurried to the second floor where Isaac and the children (Alley May, Rosemary and Esther) now gathered next to Cora who had remained in bed. As a great, ominous rumbling was heard outside, Joseph continued to plead for abandoning the home. As the house shook and then rumbled, many within began to cry and others began to pray aloud. The house then disengaged from its foundation, knocked off by the three-story pile of debris that had been created from the buildings that once comprised the neighborhood just to the South.

As the house began to capsize, Joseph seized Alley May and Rosemary by their hands and turning his back toward one of the windows, he lunged backwards breaking through the glass and shutters, taking in tow the children with him. The three managed to land on the outside wall of the house, a wall that was now parallel to the surface of the water. Isaac, somehow also managed to emerge from the house and finding some timber floated amongst the wind beaten waves.

The desperate, frantic cries of people could be heard everywhere, mingling eerily with the roar of the wind. Isaac then saw a child and swam toward her. It was his Esther. The house now completely disintegrated and melted into the sea. Isaac, Joseph, Esther, Alley May, and Rosemary treaded water until they saw a large piece of house that they climbed upon and used as a raft. Cora was found days later, buried within the massive three-story pile of debris.

CHAPTER 33

Oppressive Heat

The summer of 1900 was a blissful time for Genevieve and my self. We relished our time together. Life could not have been more wonderful. The Shop was keeping Peter and I extremely busy, and we recently had hired more help. The business was going so well that Peter had enough money saved to both expand the Print Shop as well as construct the mansion of his dreams. He had, in fact, contracted the famed architect, Nicholas Clayton, to draw plans for a most spectacular home on a lot near Broadway Ave. Construction was scheduled for the first part of 1901.

At the Hospital our research on parasitic disease was proceeding nicely. Genevieve meanwhile had started a challenging, new quilting project, and she continued to enjoy her work with the children as a volunteer at *St. Mary's Orphanage*.

As far as the weather was concerned, the summer had brought an extreme heat wave to Galveston and most of the Nation. Genevieve and I would find some reprive by going to the beach just about every Saturday. I remember reading in an August edition of **"The Galveston News"** how, many people had died in the North and the Northeast, succumbing to heat stroke. Along with the hot weather, Galveston, nonetheless, experienced its usual sudden showers flared off by the high temperature, offering some temporary relief to the oppressive heat.

I recall arriving home from work on one of those hot August days. As I entered the Villa I retrieved the handkerchief from my pocket and wiped my forehead, I found her in the parlor arranging a vase with flowers.

"Hello, my love." I said

"Hi…" she said giving me a kiss.

She saw me looking at the flower arrangement.

"Do you like it?" She inquired.

"I do! In fact the whole house looks a lot better. It's brighter and more cheerful."

She now clasped her hands around the back of my neck and gazed deep into my eyes.

"But there is something missing" She said coyly.

"What?" I pretended to be the ignorant one.

`"You know what." She playfully countered.

Pretending sudden realization I said with a chuckle "Oh… children. Well by next year God willing."

"Yes." She replied, giggling with joy.

We then shared a wonderful kiss. I so loved her to the full measure of my very being. Children would be the beautiful fruition of our love, and we both looked forward to that day.

CHAPTER 34

Signs

Looking back at the week before The Hurricane, I now can see that there were warnings as to what was to follow. At the Shop, we had an unusual misfortune of experiencing more than one press malfunction and need for repair. There also was a strange type of chaotic agitation in the air. The residents of the City seemed less patient, perhaps from the unrelenting heat. Some of the Shop customers seemed very demanding and hard to please.

At home, there were a couple of unusual instances of mishaps with our dishware. One evening while Genevieve and I were dining at home, I reached across the table for the bread and knocked my wine glass down. As it fell on the table, it surprised us by shattering forcefully, with more force than expected. The other mishap was when Mary dropped and broke a pile of dishes while she was rearranging the kitchenware in the Butler's pantry. That was the first time she ever had broken anything in the house.

During those days I also recall that Genevieve's allergies to the ragweed had been particularly intense. She had endured quite a bit of congestion and woke up that Friday, the day before the Storm, with a slight sore throat.

Friday, September 7, brought a perfect almost cloudless day. After work, Genevieve and I enjoyed a marvelous dinner at *The Tremont*. We then spent some time on the porch from which we could see the full moon rising. On Saturday, we both arose at dawn. Looking out the bedroom window, I saw a spectacular and uncommon dawn sky: It was pink in color and seemed to reflect all the colors of the rainbow.

We then each readied ourselves for the day, I for work and Genevieve for her day of volunteering at the Orphanage. I prepared some tea with honey to help soothe her sore throat before we sat down to breakfast. I kissed her before leaving and told her to be careful. It was eight in the morning, and the skies were beginning to get cloudy. A slight breeze was blowing from the north. She was scheduled to leave the Villa at 8:15.

When I arrived at the Print Shop, Peter and our three employees were already there. By midmorning, the winds, intermittent puffy gusts, had picked up slightly and it began to softly rain. Our neighbor from the newspaper stand came in and informed us that he had just seen Isaac Cline who was on his way to the Weather Bureau Office. Mr. Cline had expected a system of thundershowers to pass quickly, but he also anticipated some minor flooding. He advised the merchants to raise their goods three feet off the floor.

As flat as the Island was, occasional flooding was not uncommon. Most of the structures on Galveston were built with this in mind and had stilts or as in the case of the Villa a basement. My thoughts immediately turned to Genevieve. I did not like being without her in bad weather, and I knew how she feared storms. Immediately, we all began to do as advised and went to work.

Galveston: 1900 A Storm, A Story of Twin Flames

CHAPTER 35

The Race to the Orphanage
8th Sept, 1900

St. Mary's Orphanage on the Edge of the Gulf of Mexico

We worked the rest of the morning and past noon to get all our valuables above the advised three-foot level. Although the wind and rain would wax and wane, the low-lying clouds now appeared more ominous. Peter had placed a call to Karina. She along with the children was on their way to her Mother's house located a few blocks from *Ursuline Academy*. Her Mother, Annabelle, was convalescing at her own house and was too ill to be moved. I tried to place a call to the Orphanage but the line was dead. At around 1:30 p.m., a tremendous blast of wind erupted through the Strand. It was accompanied by a deafening crash.

As we all ran outside to determine the source of the explosion, we were met by the sight *Ritter's Cafe* in a state of destruction. The wind had peeled off the roof causing the contents, heavy printing presses as well as office furniture from the second floor, to collapse onto the restaurant below. All of us dashed to the scene, people were moaning with pain, blood covered the floor. It looked like a bomb had exploded inside.

Later I would learn that among the five killed there was Stanley G. Spencer, a steamship agent for the **North German Lloyd Lines**. Stanley was a valued client at the Print Shop, placing regular orders for his company. He was having lunch with Richard Lord, a traffic manager for the cotton exporter McFadden & Brother, when the tragedy struck.

At the Café, we were joined by others merchants who had likewise heard the blast.

"I'm going to help here. Then I will go to Annabelle's house." Peter yelled over the wind.

"I'm going to get Genevieve." I shouted back.

"Yes take care if her. Be careful my brother."

"You also."

With that I ran to the back of the Print Shop, where I located my horse and buggy, and unfolded the retractable hood so that I would I have some protection against the rain. I then directed my horse west on Broadway. There I saw a parade of refugees making their way toward the safer area of the central city. Some warned me to turn back, but I proceeded forward through thigh deep water that was now littered with tree limbs, pieces of wood, clothes, and thousands of toads.

As I approached the Gulf, the crashing waves sounded like deafening canon fire. When I first witnessed the Gulf, my jaw dropped. I blinked to make sure that the rain getting in my eyes was not playing tricks with my vision. I heard my horse becoming frightened, snorting and neighing loudly.

"My God…"

At the horizon, the Gulf looked like a great, gray wall of water, fifty foot high. It seemed to be slowly creeping toward the Island. It gave me the sensation that the Island was slowly sinking into the bedrock below. The angry swells that pounded the beach were foams of agitated phosphorescence.

I whipped the horse onward and soon was at the Orphanage were the surf was now crashing only yards away from the lower floor. Finding a tree a safe distance from the building, I tied my horse to it and dashed inside.

I burst through the front door.

"Genevieve, Genevieve…" I called out.

It seemed that everybody was upstairs. I ran up the stairs. Hearing my voice, I heard Genevieve call out.

"Uri. We're here!"

I rushed into the dining room where everyone was gathered. We rushed into each other's arms.

"I was so worried. I tried calling, but the phone lines were dead. *Ritter's Café* was devastated by the winds. I need to take you home."

I now looked at Sister Tracy and added.

"Sister, we must all leave immediately."

"Uri, it's much too dangerous. Beside, we only have five buggies in the stables. "

"If we pile eight to a buggy, we can take the youngest forty-eight children with us when you include my buggy." I pleaded.

"We stay here where it's safe." Insisted Sister Tracey.

Exasperatedly, I said. "Sister I just saw a wall of water at the horizon. It's making its way toward us. It wasn't easy getting here, and the longer we wait the harder it will be to get back. Let's take the youngest with us and go back to my house. It's close to the high point of the Island. We are bound to run into others along the way who can help us rescue whoever remains behind."

"The children can't be out in this kind of weather, Uri. We don't have enough buggies to move everyone all at once. We have faith in God. With God's will, the storm shall pass quickly."

I now turned to Genevieve.

"What can we say to convince her?"

"Sister, please let us take as many as possible. We will find help along the way and to evacuate the rest of the children and other Sisters" Genevieve implored.

I could hear the great concern mixed with sadness in her voice.

"I don't want to leave them here." She said in a shaky whisper, as though speaking to herself.

Sister Tracy then approached Genevieve and in a gesture of reassurance placed a hand on each of Genevieve's shoulders.

"If Uri is that set on leaving, please both of you go with God. We will remain here trusting our lives to Him."

With great reluctance, we finally acquiesced.

The Sisters, Genevieve and I then proceeded to escort all ninety-three children to the Chapel. Because the children had become frightened at what I had said about the wall of water in the Gulf, Sister Tracy fetched some clothesline and instructed the other Sisters to tie one end to each of their own waists and tie six to eight children to themselves, using the rest of the line.

The pounding of the waves now seemed to shake the building, further terrifying the children. The Sisters then led the children in song, singing *"Queen of the Waves."* During this entire time, I quietly pleaded and begged Genevieve to leave. She finally relented once she saw that the children had been pacified by the music. With tears welling in her eyes, we left.

Once outside, I saw a dramatic difference in terms of the Storm's intensity. I could tell that the barometric pressure had dropped as my eardrums felt as they were popping outward. The wind gusts were probably up to forty-five mile per hour, and heavy curtains of rain flew down from above. We treaded through water that was just below the waist. I helped her into the buggy, and directed the horse back to town. Riding back through water littered with all sorts of debris, and with the wind and rain screeching from above, unnerved my horse. He began rolling his eyes and jerking his head about wildly.

As we sloshed along the path that led back, there finally was a break in the weather. The velocity of the wind and intensity of rain had slowed. Later I would learn that this lull was the result of us experiencing the weaker part of the hurricane between the bands of clouds. The harrowing journey was more like traveling in a boat than a buggy. It was as though we navigating in the canals of Venice in the midst of some freakish storm. Although floating debris such as crates, planks of wood, clothes and even a squealing pig would at times impede our path, we none the less made good progress. Reaching the west end of the city, my best estimation was that it was now around 4:00 p.m., although the swift-moving, dark sky above made it seem much later. At any rate I knew I had to get us to the safety of the Villa as soon as possible.

We had made it to Broadway perhaps less than two miles from

home when the Storm took a violent turn for the worse. A tremendous blast of wind ripped the buggy hood clean off, and sent it flying backwards and out of sight. The relentless, full gale force wind now smashed cold horizontal, rain into our faces. It felt as though tiny splinters of wood were striking us. We now heard desperate shrieks, crying out for help by others caught in the Storm, but with the darkness closing in it was difficult to see from where these cries originated.

Slogging forward trough the river-swollen street, the wind, eerily whistled through the passage created by the buildings lining each side of the street. I noticed that the wind had shifted and was blowing from the East. It now struck us head-on, further slowing our progress. Massive jagged streaks of lighting ripped through the sky kindling it as though it was midday, immediately followed by tremendous, ear-spitting peals of thunder.

My horse was now extremely spooked and was neighing and snorting uncontrollably. We heard the snapping of wood just as we passed an electric pole. It fell behind us just as we passed through. The buggy now came to a halt. I hit the horse as it tried to lunge forward, with no avail.

"We're stuck... I'm going to get out and push the buggy." I yelled above the roar of the wind.

Splashing down into the rushing water, the current suddenly tugged me backward, and I was in danger of totally being dragged away.

"Uri... Uri!" Genevieve yelled, filled with panic.

Seeing the back wheel of the buggy I lunged to grab it.

"I'm O.K..."

I now positioned myself behind the buggy.

"When I say "Now" hit the horse with the whip... Now!"

Genevieve struck the animal and yelled at the horse.

"Come on! ....Come on!!"

With tremendous effort, we finally managed to get the buggy moving. Using my hands and with the aid of the strength of my arms, I made my way to the side of the buggy where Genevieve helped me back into the seat. Assuming control of the horse, I lashed the poor animal ruthlessly urging the half dead creature onward.

The water was now at chest level and the fearsome winds were rocketing roof shingles, parts of trees, poles, and other debris into the air. We saw a horse, impaled at the neck by an air borne missile, sink into the water. Realizing our dire situation, I, like a mad man, beat my horse mercilessly, trying to move us forward more quickly. Through glimpses provided by lightning igniting the darkening sky, I clearly saw that my horse's mouth was now completely covered with foam. Soon he collapsed into the water.

"No.. No.. We can't stay out here." I wailed.

I looked around. We were in the warehouse district near the Cotton Presses. A half block away I spotted a solid brick, three-story warehouse.

"We need to go there!" I yelled, pointing it to Genevieve.

Clouds of debris were now traveling through the air like streaking kites, and in the far distance I saw some bricks from the top floor of one of the large buildings float off like tiny feathers. I helped Genevieve out of the buggy into chest deep water where we used a streetcar cable to pull ourselves toward the direction of the warehouse. A large wave suddenly knocked us backward, almost dislodging us from the cable. Fortunately, we again secured our grip and moved forward to the elevated walkway of the warehouse.

As we approached the front door, I heard Genevieve scream.

"Aggh!!"

"What happened?

"Something flying through the air hit me." She was panting with anguish.

I guided Genevieve into the recess of the warehouse. The shelter of the recess provided some reprieve from the raging tempest that now pounded the raindrops into the wall of the warehouse with such force that each drop exploded into pixels of light. With another bolt of lightning, I saw a large gash on the upper part of her right arm. It was bleeding profusely. Tearing off a piece of my shirt, I created a bandage that I tightly tied around her arm to stop the bleeding.

"Hold on. I'll get us inside."

I tried to open the door. Locked.

"Damn, it." I screamed.

The water now was beginning to rise again. I used my shoulder to ram in the door. After a number of hard blows, the door flew open. With the accumulation of water from the outside, we were swept into the interior of the warehouse. I grabbed Genevieve's hand and quickly located the stairs. As we made our way to the safety of he second floor, the velocity of the wind increased, sounding like a thousand shrieking devils.

"How's the arm?"

"It hurts… The storm, it's too strong."

"We're going to make it!" I affirmed, holding her tightly.

Her thoughts now turned to the family.

"I pray Mother and Father… Peter and his are all right."

All I could do was shake my head in agreement.

We now huddled together in the center of the second floor. Soon we heard the rush of water.

"Is that…more water?" She asked.

I went to the stair well and peaked down.

"It looks like the ocean moved in. We'll stay here for now. I don't want us to go to the third floor if we don't have to. The wind is strong enough to rip the roof off." I yelled back at the top of my lungs.

Trapped now in the warehouse during the worst part of the Storm, time barely moved. It seemed as though everything was happening in slow motion. After a period of time, we heard the exploding of timber above us.

"It's being ripped off." I shouted in her ear.

The wind had become deafening, and it felt as though our eardrums were about to explode. We crouched down on the floor as the windows on the windward side of the warehouse exploded inward, spraying glass like shot gun fire. We could hear the contents on the third floor being dragged across the room and out of the building.

On the second floor, we now could feel a strong vacuum of wind traveling through the room. As this force increased, I clutched Genevieve tightly. We were being dragged toward the stairway that led to the third floor.

"Whatever happens, hold on to me!" I shouted into her ear.

"I will!"

Right before being sucked by the monstrous wind to the third floor, I spotted a pipe anchored to the floor. With Genevieve holding onto me with all her strength, I clenched my hands onto this tube. In the meantime, boxes, crates and furniture were all flying past us as they shot to the upper floor.

"Look out!!" Genevieve screamed.

She had spotted a large heavy box coming right at us. I ducked and simultaneously manipulated our position in space just as the box passed within inches of my head. With this shift in position, I lost my grip on the pipe, placing us in danger of being carried out by the wind. Genevieve, realizing the danger we were in, lunged for the pipe with her free hand, securing us to where we were.

The enormous winds began to die down. Exhausted and breathless I whispered to her.

"I couldn't hold on much longer."

We rolled onto the floor completely exhausted. After half drifting into unconsciousness, I made a makeshift bed out of some packing blankets where we plunged into the blackness of sleep.

CHAPTER 36

The Morning After

With the first rays of dawn I opened my eyes and looking through the blown out windows of the warehouse from my supine position, I saw the sky. It was a most beautiful cantaloupe color. The air was strangely still with not even a breeze stirring. Immediately my attention turned to Genevieve who was lying next to me. I froze as I saw her face. It was flushed and tinged with crimson.

"Genevieve..." She slightly stirred.

"Genevieve..." I said more emphatically.

"Hmm?..." She wrinkled her brow.

I reached out and touched her forehead confirming what I already knew. I then examined the wound on her arm, taking off the bandage. I held in a gasp as I closely examined it for the first time. It was a nasty injury about four inches across, deep and with jagged edges. Parts of it extended into the muscle. Even after all these hours it still was oozing some blood and plasma, now that it was exposed. I realized with great apprehension that the wound needed prompt treatment. It required disinfection and stitches.

My thoughts raced back to how Genevieve's allergies this past week had caused much sneezing and sinus congestion, and how she had awakened to a mild sore throat on Saturday morning. No doubt this had weakened her immune system, leaving her more vulnerable to the complications of such an injury. I needed to get her to the Hospital.

"Darling..." I was now shaking her awake.

She opened her eyes. Her tired eyes brightened to see me.

"How do you feel?"

"Tired.... I am very hot." She said wiping the film of perspiration from her forehead.

"You are running a fever... I need to get you to the Hospital and get that arm treated."

I now helped her to her feet, and I braced her weight with my arm my around her waist. She groaned slightly as she slung her left uninjured arm over my shoulder. Arm in arm we preceded slowly down the steps. Reaching the bottom floor, we treaded through a six-inch mush of sandy silt. All the contents within the lower floor of the warehouse had been pummeled by the rushing tidal surge into piles of chaotic destruction against the back wall of the warehouse. We now walked through the door and into open.

There were piles of debris everywhere. As we proceeded forward, my mind was preoccupied by the solitary goal of getting Genevieve to the Hospital. We plodded slowly through large puddles and around mounds of rubble, fallen electric poles, and parts of buildings. I even seem to recall seeing some lifeless bodies strewn along our way.

    I vaguely recollect people wandering throughout the streets, straggling in stunned silence. Occasionally, sharp, painful wails would break the silence, cries of indescribable hurt and agony. We passed the City Water Works, a complete wreck except for its large chimney. We passed the *Tremont Hotel* where many people where milling in and out. Because of all the barriers caused by the Storm, the normal forty-five minute walk took an eternity, many hours. Despite the difficulty, I do not remember Genevieve complaining even once. Finally, at Strand St. we headed east where a large procession of people was walking toward *Old Red*.

    The left third of the roof of the hospital had been completely blown off as had most of the windows. Covered in muddy slime, we hobbled up the steps behind a line of people like survivors returning from the front lines of a war zone. There were bloodied, mangled people everywhere. Many of the injured were barely clothed and what remained of their garments was tattered to shreds. I saw people with crudely applied tourniquets. Some barely hobbled in. Others totally unconscious perhaps no longer alive were carried in. Entering the main hall, we saw a mass of humanity. Above the commotion I could hear painful moans and crying. I looked for a place for Genevieve to sit, but every bench was occupied. I gently slid her to the floor.

    "I'll be right back."

    She gave me a small smile and nodded.

    I made my way up to the Research room where I found a chair and made my way through the crowded halls, back to Genevieve.

    "Here..." I said as I positioned the chair and then helped her to sit.

    "I'm really thirsty." She said softly.

    "Let me see where I can find some water."

    After discovering that no running water could be found anywhere within the Hospital, I dashed outside with a pitcher I found in the dining hall. I then went to the back of the building where I knew that emergency cisterns were stored. Hospital employees were supervising the rationing of water to those who needed it. They allowed me to fill my pitcher. I ran back and holding the pitcher to Genevieve's lips, she quenched her thirst.

    The day was beginning to get hot, and the throngs of people, so crowded together magnified the temperature. The smell of sweat and blood as well as the stench wafting in from the outside was making everybody nauseous, especially the sick and injured like Genevieve. Having settled Genevieve so that she would be more comfortable, I told her I would try to find Dr. Bernstein. After searching what seemed like countless rooms filled with the maimed, sick, and dying I finally found him exiting from one of the patient convalescent suites.

"Dr. Bernstein..." I was trying to catch my breath.

"Genevieve has been badly injured."

"Can she walk?" his voice seemed far away.

"Why, yes..."

"Then it will have to wait." he interrupted me abruptly. "I'm headed down to surgery. Many amputations are awaiting.."

With that he hurriedly walked away. My stomach turned, as I stood there uncertain as what to do. From everything I had learned, I certainly knew that time was an enemy when dealing with infections. I had to do something. Then it came to me. I dashed up to the research room where I opened a cabinet and grabbed a bottle of hydrogen peroxide and ethanol. Next I looked for the cleanest towel I could find as well as for a pair of scissors. With my supplies in hand, I raced downstairs.

CHAPTER 37

At the Hospital

Reaching Genevieve sitting on the chair, her eyes closed and resting her head on the wall for support, I cut the makeshift bandage exposing the unsightly wound. The edges were now more inflamed and the dried blood within the gash now oozed some pus. She winced as I cleaned the injury with a peroxide-soaked piece of cloth I had cut from the towel. After meticulously cleaning the area, I proceeded to wrap the arm in new bandages, which I made from the towel. I felt her forehead, and could tell that she was growing warmer. Soaking the remaining towel with water, I placed it on her head.

"Thanks, you always take such good care of me." She smiled softly.

As the day wore on, I occasionally would glance outside through the Hospital window and at one point realized that dead bodies loaded on wagons were arriving at the Hospital where they were they were being taken to a temporary morgue that has been set up in the basement. My thoughts turned to Peter, Karina, and the children. I prayed that they all made it safely through the Storm.

Genevieve and I shared some grits that was prepared by the Hospital staff, and we watched day turn to night. With absolutely no electricity, the staff and Doctors were using candles and kerosene lanterns as they continued working throughout the night.

Finally, the next day, Genevieve was given a room that was shared with a number of other patients. Privacy was created by the use of partitions. I stayed by her side the entire time and regularly disinfected the worsening wound and bandaged it with fresh cloth.

When her parents showed up at the Hospital, my thoughts again turned to Peter, Karina, and the children. Mrs. Parker said that she and her husband had managed to survive by abandoning their own house in favor of a friend's who lived uptown. The friend's house was a much sturdier brick one. This saved their lives because the Parker residence as well as their entire neighborhood had been completely destroyed.

I asked them about Peter and Karina and the children, but neither one of them had seen my family. They did know, however, that the neighborhood where Karina's Mother lived, and where I presumed that Peter had been during the Storm, had also been completely obliterated.

Dr. Burnstein finally entered the room to examine Genevieve, who seemed to be at least stable at that point. He measured her temperature, 102 degrees. He then used a stethoscope to listen to her heart, and lungs. When he unwrapped the wound, I saw concern register on his face.

"I have been treating it with hydrogen peroxide and ethanol three times a day." I said.

He next palpated the lymph nodes under her arm, causing her to emit a slight painful moan. He then palpated the lymph nodes of the upper left leg.

"Inflamed..." He referred to the lymph nodes and looked at me. He motioned to talk to me in private.

"Uri, the infection has spread into the blood." He whispered.

"Septicemia." escaped my lips.

"Early... Amputation is not a good option in these cases."

"Amputation?" I said in disbelief.

He put his hand on my shoulder.

"I will return shortly to disinfect the wound and then apply stitches." He related with hopeful assurance.

As he left, I gloomy, sickening dejection overcame me. How could this be happening? I wondered to myself over and over.

A short time later, Dr. Bernstein returned with a surgical kit. As he administered the chloroform vapor that served as a central nervous system anesthesia, I held Genevieve's left hand in mine. As soon as the drug had taken effect, he went to work. As he proceeded, I assisted him by handing him the instruments that he requested. First he thoroughly cleaned the wound with gauze soaked in hydrogen peroxide. He then inserted the needle attached to a syringe, deep into the wound from which he aspirated thick creamy yellow green pus that had accumulated within. Using another syringe filled with phenol, he injected the solution into the tissue and blotted the excess with more gauze. Finally, he sewed the wound together and applied a bandage over it.

At first, Genevieve's condition seemed to stabilize with her temperature hovering around 102 degrees. She would even smile at some of the silly comments I made as I attempted to lighten the mood. She enjoyed her parents company, and they were there with us everyday.

She remained beautiful, dressed as she was in the hospital gown and my locket, which she insisted keeping around her neck. The illness could not diminish her attractiveness, and though the disease so ravaged her body, it could not take away her grace. I insisted on disinfecting the wound and changing her bandages, a procedure that I repeated six times a day. The wound, however, never looked any better and as much as I tried to deny it, started looking worse.

Days later, I saw Dr. Bernstein's countenance fall as he looked at the thermometer. It now read 106 degrees. He listened to her heart and then lungs. He palpated all the lymph nodes of her entire body.

In the privacy of a corner of the room he briefed my on the findings. I braced myself before the words came out.

"Uri..." he began very slowly.

"The infection is not getting any better, but much worse. Every lymph node of the body is involved, and there is some fluid in the lungs."

"You can't be telling me this." I demanded. "Surely, there is something more we can do." my voice trailed off breaking up at the end.

After some contemplation, Dr. Bernstein replied.

"I could try the diphtheria antitoxin, on the outside chance that it could have some effect on the septicemia."

"Please do that, Doctor... I can't lose her." a large lump formed in my throat.

" I will also order some more aspirin for the fever." He informed before leaving the room.

Later that day, he administered the antitoxin. It had no effect. As much I loathed to concede it, we all knew that the inevitable would soon come. I tried my best to conceal my sorrow from her, but she knew all too well. Since our first meeting there in the Print Shop, I always had been aware that she knew my inner most thoughts. The fluid in her lungs was now causing bouts of cough, which was somewhat, relieved by a cough elixir. Even now, so near the end she still had her grace that was both sublime and admirable.

When she was awake, she would look at me, and I saw sadness, more for my pain and anguish, than for the end that she was facing. Infused with this melancholy was a cognition that required no spoken words. This cognition was a telepathic connection that she and I shared. Even just lying there asleep or unconscious, as was the case for much of the time during her last days, I knew that she absolutely treasured every minute that we were sharing together, perhaps now more than ever, with an end so imminent. That reality and realization made every second, as agonizing as it was, so much more precious.

> *September 18, 1900: Her breathing rate had markedly increased and her temperature climbed to 107 degrees.*

At last the tragic, unthinkable day was here. I waited outside the room while James and Stephanie talked to her inside. Crestfallen, James emerged from the room followed shortly by Stephanie whose eyes were swollen from crying.

"Uri, she's asking for you." James turned his head to Stephanie and continued.

"I'm going to step outside a few moments. I need some fresh air."

After James walked away, Stephanie spoke with the most heartfelt honesty that I had ever seen from her. Sincerity brought on by tremendous guilt.

"Uri, I want to apologize for the past... You gave her true happiness. My poor behavior..." She began crying again.

"I embarrassed to say, came from my own jealousy. She did not settle for less than the one who was perfect for her."

With that she gave me a hug and whispered.

"Now go to her."

I crept into the room and saw my Genevieve, eyes closed, the fingers of her left hand wrapped tightly around the heart locket. Approaching the bedside, she sensed my presence and forced her eyes open. Even now her eyes brightened, so happy to see me.

"Hello, my Love... My Princess." I said as I stroked her hot forehead. I now took her hand in mine. Large tears rolled down my cheeks.

"I'm sorry, I didn't leave the Shop earlier before the Storm got so severe."

"You were magnificent. It struck totally without warning." She paused before continuing.

"When I'm gone, I want you to promise to take care of yourself."

I choked with tears.

"Don't talk like that."

Aching sadness fell across her face. In her final moments she could only think of me.

"Please promise me..."

"How can I go on without you?"

"I will always be near... As strange as it may sound, I feel that in some way we were together even before we met."

Tears now poured down my face.

"I know... You have always been a part of me."

"I am at peace to have been with you... finally together..."

"I love you..." I said.

"I will love you always..."

On my knees bent over the side of the bed, I cradled her in my arms until the last sigh of breath escaped from her lips. Sharp daggers of pain tore apart my heart as I clutched her in my arms refusing to let go. The nauseating pain I felt was unimaginable... cold, absolutely forlorn, pitch black. Leaving me in a place of ugly dread, a place of utter solitary abandonment. I could feel my body shaking as waves of uncontrollable sobs, overcame my being.

There I stayed for a long time.

Galveston: 1900 A Storm, A Story of Twin Flames
CHAPTER 38

Wandering Through the Devastation

Too Many to Bury: Burning the Dead on Funeral Pyres

I walked out of the Hospital in a murky fog, dazed like the walking dead. Not intentionally planning to go anywhere in particular. I proceeded east where the Wharfs were. The landscape there was a sea of wreckage with broken timbers everywhere. Where the many, stout piers once stood were now only supporting stilts sticking out of the water. In the air, I detected the smell of rot and old decay. A group of men were clearing debris from around a lopsided sail ship that had been pushed ashore. Beyond this, I saw the large Steamer, ***S.S. Alamo***, lodged on top of *Mallory Wharf*. On the far west side where the Wharf ended, I saw some men throwing indiscernible things onto a bonfire.

I continued down to Strand Street with a vague awareness that the Print Shop was there. Every shop was damaged with roofs ripped off, gaping holes, broken windows. Some appeared to have been looted. I passed *The Gulf, Colorado, and Santa Fe Terminal* and saw its rectangular corner steeple, jagged and half of it missing. It looked as though some giant had taken a bite out of it.

I came upon *Ritter's Café*. It was almost unrecognizable having completely collapsed from the top. What was once the second floor façade was now lying as a mountain of bricks on the sidewalk. Within the building were a group of men working to clear the heavy printing presses that had collapsed from the second floor. I briefly stole a glance across at our store and saw that it was severely wrecked. I turned away, not wanting to see more, and came upon a fellow merchant.

"Mr. Samuels." I called out.

"Uri…" His weak voice trailed off.

"Have you seen Peter?"

"The last time I saw him was when I closed my shop. He was helping the injured at Ritter's. I'm sorry."

I trudged ahead dragging my feet through the half-foot of muddy slime that seemed to be everywhere. At Tremont Street, I paused as something caught my eye. This was the very street where I first saw Genevieve riding in the buggy with her Mother. That day now seemed an eternity, perhaps even another lifetime ago. Looking a few yards away at the very corner where Genevieve had rode out of sight was a pile of debris upon which lay a doll. I clutched my chest in torment at the pain I felt within my heart. Moving next to the pile, I now peered at the doll more closely. Although she was covered in mud, she was beautiful, her unblinking eyes looking up at mine. Agonizing, I turned away and decided to find the place where Peter and his family was last, as far as I knew, on that cursed day.

Bath Avenue was a wreck with virtually every house damaged,

some totally collapsed, others completely gone. The stench of putrefaction and human waste seemed to be getting worse. Throughout the Avenue were crews of men, working in silence, laboring to clear debris from the road. I saw dead dogs, cats, pigs, and chickens heaped on piles and within piles of rubbish. The stifling heat cooking their bloated bodies. Further down I passed a wandering cow and horse. Now ownerless, they looked at me with hopeful, hunger filled eyes. Even animals had a desire for someone to return them to a life with some semblance of normalcy.

I was not that person. I had been transformed. I was now more like a cocaine addict. A being subsisting within the mind-body disassociated state that that drug induces. A walking skeleton animated by self-moving muscles. A Rip Van Winkle awakening a hundred years later to a totally different world.

Throughout my trek I passed many others who calmly ambulated with almost zombie like demeanor. I surmised that they were still in a state of shock mixed with denial. Occasionally, a piercing shriek or cry would break the silence, like a dagger slicing through the hot dense, still air.

Out in the distance, I now saw an enormous mound like a mountain cutting through the city, extending east to west. The details of this pile emerged as I approached L Street. It was what had been the Gulf side of the city. A two story pile of crushed houses, parts of houses, streetcars, timber, trees, furniture, dishes, clothes, outhouses, and the corpses of people and animals. The stench of rotting flesh and excrement was overwhelming. On top of this mountain of rubbish were many men removing debris, trying to dig out the dead.

Beyond the pile my mouth dropped, I was in open land that was once totally filled with houses. Peter, Karina's Mother, Isaac Cline, Dr. Young, fellow residents, and my customers. It was as though the ground had been swept clean by a giant broom.
To my right, with the heavily littered *Garten Verein* behind it, I saw the *Venetian*, *Gothic Ursuline Academy* heavily damaged, windows blown out, much of its roof gone.

In the clearing just ahead, I spotted Sandra Brown, a client from the Shop, and approached her.

" Mrs. Brown, have you seen Peter or his family?"

"No, I'm afraid I haven't. I have been looking for my husband for days." She began sobbing.

Regaining some composure she continued.

"He's vanished without a trace."

I don't recall responding to her, but my feet carried me forward.

To my right was *Rosenburg's Women's Home* extensively damaged, bricks lying in piles, its roof seared off. The Women's Home had faired pretty well compared to its neighbor *The Bath Avenue Public School*. The Gulf facing quarter portion of this building had imploded with its third floor classroom cascading down to the ground. On this third floor were desks that were bolted to the floor, nicely displayed like toys on some giant slide. When I looked right, I saw a community of large white tents, where the homeless now dwelled.

At the beach, my jaw dropped again. Where there was once sand, there now was surf. A full two to three blocks of Island were now gone, seemingly carved out of existence by some giant scalpel. Directly ahead in the water, were stilts that stuck out of the surf, the only remains of *Murdoch's* To my left, the tall chimney, the only remnant from the burned down *Beach Hotel*, was now reduced to a pile of bricks, the lap of the waves bathing them in frothy foam. To my right where Olympia once stood were only stilts protruding from the surf. They now looked like grave markers for some ancient ruin, testifying to something grand that once stood there so long ago.

Off to either side, I now saw bonfires around which groups of men gathered. The fires seemed to extend on the beach as far as my eye could see. I walked to the nearest bonfire and saw a group of colored men soaking corpses with oil. I stared in horror as I noted the gruesome details. Morbid images that still haunt my mind to this day. The dead were almost unrecognizable, bloated, many covered with dried blood, eyes popping out of their skulls, bodies turning purple. Some of the bodies were dressed in tattered clothes that had been ripped to shreds by the extreme winds. Others were completely naked. Most had maggot infested, disfiguring lacerations. One was eviscerated with her bowels prolapsed out.

All of them were overcome with rigor mortis. Some of these corpses held their hands overhead as if trying to protect themselves. Looking more closely at these hand expressions, I thought they could also represent gestures of supplication, last-ditch efforts to pray.

As much as I wanted to turn away, I compelled myself to discern if any of the victims were from my own family. As the smell of ghastly purification overwhelmed by nostrils, I began to retch. Nothing more than bile came out, as I had not eaten in a long time. None seemed recognizable as anyone familiar. The colored men now heaved the bodies one at a time onto the funeral pyre. Overseeing the operation was a middle aged white man with shotgun in hand. The way he directed the firearm in the direction of the colored men told me that their participation in the exercise was completely coerced.

"Pardon me, sir... Why are you doing this?" I asked in a croaked voice.

The white man with a heavy Texas drawl turned to me and related without emotion.

"We're burning the bodies of the dead. The Relief Committee ordered the dead to be burned to prevent an epidemic. We dumped the bodies at sea days ago, but most of them just floated back."

"Oh..." It was the only word that could escape from my mouth.

I slogged east along the beach, passing a couple of more pyres on the way, refusing to look at them directly. Reaching 20th Street, I trudged back toward town. By this time the mud and slime that caked my pants had made my steps more laborious. Passing the *City Street Railway Power House*, which supplied electric power to the streetcars, I saw that it was a total ruin. Every wall had collapsed. The foundation was mass of bricks interspersed with the large wheels that were used to turn the generators.

Up ahead, I saw the Opera House with an immense gaping hole exposed at its rear half. I thought that I was going off my trolley, as I seemed to hear a few cheerful notes coming from the orchestra pit. Up ahead, I came upon *City Hall*. The once magnificent white Renaissance structure was severely damaged with its roof sliced off and the cupola above the left turret missing.

As I hobbled past the lower floor that once housed the meat market, a group of officers, all armed and on horseback were approaching from Market Street. As they drew closer, I saw them regard me carefully and with suspicion. Determining that I was harmless, they quickly rode away. I realized that Martial Law had been declared. Proceeding a short distance down Market Street, I passed *Justus Schott Druggist Shop* and observed that in addition to the damage sustained by the Storm, it had been completely looted. Ambling southward past *Ball High School* with some of its walls collapsed, I then hobbled past City Park. Its once tranquil grounds were dotted with a community of tents and inhabited by homeless residents milling about.

Finally, I arrived at our Villa. By now my vision was glazed and my senses were utterly useless. I more felt, than saw, that the Villa was extensively damaged, but I did not care. I clutched the gate and then slid down to the sidewalk, a clump of tortured pain and defeat.

On the ground, I curled into a ball and closed my eyes. I was a dog beaten into submission. Alone and condemned without any trace of hope whatsoever. ***Wanting it all to go away. Half hoping that it was all just a*** *monstrous, sinister lie. Just one false, gigantic nightmare….*

When I finally opened my eyes, I beheld the iron-gates before me, but now they were unfocused and blurry. For a brief moment I thought that these must be the gates of Hell. As they started spinning, I faded into total blackness.

Galveston: 1900 A Storm, A Story of Twin Flames

CHAPTER 39

Haunted

Undulations of misery and heartache racked my body, as real and immediate as the day of Genevieve's death. Reaching into my jacket pocket and retrieving a handkerchief, I wiped the trail of tears that had rolled down my face. I then put my glasses back on and glancing up above, saw a sky that was dreary and overcast.

Tragically, we never found Peter, Karina, or any of the children, not even a corpse that could be mourned. I could only surmise that the last moments of their lives were similar to that of the Cline family given the proximity of the houses as The Storm struck. I am forever haunted by images of them, glimpses in my mind, of seeing them buried beneath the immense pile of debris that faced the Gulf.

I was informed later by Dr. Young that Hank's corpse was found buried beneath a pile of bricks that was once *Lucas Terrace Apartments*, a complex that stood on the East end of Broadway Avenue a few blocks from the Gulf. The back half of his skull was missing severed clean off by flying debris.

In the weeks that followed, I remember over hearing numerous conversations amongst the Island's residents as to how such a thing could happen to such a beautiful city. Blame was laid variously to such people as the atheists, the Jews, the homosexuals, and even the Ladies of the Night who worked at the seedier saloons. When overhearing such talk, the word "hubris" would most often come to my mind. Retribution, for the bygone lashes of the taskmaster, was the other thought that less frequently entered my contemplation.

Twelve years later I remember the commotion that resulted when a similar tragedy befell a spectacular, jewel of a Ship crossing the North Atlantic. Again the word "hubris" entrenched in my thoughts.

In the end, the "why" could never be explained. In the end, as a general rule, for those who lost little or nothing there was Faith.... and for those of us who lost everything there was only Doubt.

The Great Hurricane had consumed me at every level possible. I had become a mere silhouette of my former self. For me there could never be any peace of mind. A thick, morbid loneliness, hanging like an albatross around my neck, enveloped me like a fog. To try to forget, to try to escape the anguish I felt, was like to attempt to harvest the wind. The only intervals of brief reprieve, when I temporarily forgot, were when I absorbed myself in my research.

Just as I had dedicated the rest of my life to research, for the singular purpose of eradicating the sepsis that had taken what was so precious to me, I also was compelled to know more about the Cursed Storm itself. I had to learn what it was doing as it unleashed itself upon us on that apocalyptic day.

What remained within me was an overpowering, nagging feeling that if I had known more; I could have saved my Genevieve. This quest, riddled with guilt, as to what I could have or should have done differently as well as the crusade for an antibiotic was what had transmogrified me into the being I had now become.

I subscribed to *"The Quarterly Journal of the Royal Meteorological Society"*, looking for any articles relating to hurricanes. In an issue years later, I found an article that was republished from a memoir by Ben C. Stuart, a writer at *"The Galveston Daily News"*. The article recounted the horrific details:

> *Ironically, that morning a large crowd of residents had gathered at the beach along The Midway to witness waves that "were spectacular and beautiful." The crowd began fleeing around 10:30 a.m. when the swells, so large and destructive, began dismantling The Bathhouses and the ramshackle structures along The Midway. The maximum sustained wind velocity occurred between 5:15 p.m. and 7:00 p.m. and was estimated to be 120 mph with wind gusts of perhaps 200 mph. This force is estimated to be 152 lbs. of pressure/square inch or thirty tons of pressure on a house wall. The total wind duration was close to 16 hours and was directed as follows: 10:00 am from the North, 2:00 p.m. from the Northeast, 4:30 p.m. from the East, 7:30 p.m. from the South.*
>
> *At the height of wind velocity, bricks were ripped from buildings and were reported by eyewitnesses to float off into the air like feathers. Large flying debris became lethal projectiles decapitating and eviscerating humans and animals alike. There were even reports of small objects such as splinters piercing bodies and penetrating eyes. Shingles were turned into missiles, and entire roofs were lifted into the*

air. Even a train from Galveston was later found washed ashore on the Texas mainland. The wagon bridge spanning the Bay was completely destroyed as well as the three railroad causeways, the later damaged when the S.S. Roma broke loose from its ties at the Wharf and was hurled wildly into the Bay.

Barometric pressure, as registered at the Levy Building, plunged to 27.49 in hg., the lowest ever recorded to that date and one of the lowest ever to be recorded in weather history. 2,636 housed were completely destroyed with another 1000 wrecked beyond repair. Within the two-story wreckage that spanned the Gulf side of the city were more than 3,000 corpses. On the shores of the Bay were found another 500 with many picked to bits by buzzards.

Another 500 were swept out to sea by the tidal surge. 6,000 Galveston residents were confirmed dead. Another 1000 to 1200 on the island to the west. On the Texas mainland at least another 1000. The total carnage was at least 8,000 with estimates up to 12,000.

There were reports of residents who survived the onslaught by clinging onto stout trees where they rode out The Storm accompanied by snakes that had also sought refuge amongst the branches. Two who survived by such means were two boys from the Orphanage, the only ones who were not buried under the debris of the place they called home. What probably saved them was that somehow they failed to be tied to any of the Sisters. One of these boys who survived recounted that during the last harrowing moments, one of the Sisters grabbed two small, terrified children into her arms and reassuring them promised to not let them go. Many days later two of the Sisters were found on the Texas main land, having been washed across the Bay. One of these two Sisters, bound with rigor mortis, had within her arms the corpses of two small children. She had fulfilled her vow that she would never let go. A vow that not even death could break. There were other miraculous tales of survival such as that of sixteen-year-old Anna Delz. She was washed onto the Texas mainland and feared dead until she made her way back to her family in Galveston one week later.

"Dead Gang Members", who in many cases were colored people, ingested with plenty of whiskey and persuaded at gunpoint to work on the gruesome task of search and disposal, retrieved bodies. When it was realized that there were too many corpses to bury, the dead were loaded onto funeral barges on Saturday the 10th. Once loaded onto these barges, they were then weighted down with heavy objects such as rail ties. Most floated back the following day, and the funeral pyres were commenced on Wednesday.

These fires burned for many weeks after the disaster. The two-story mountain of debris was also burned in sections along with the remaining corpses buried within. Fever and dysentery were rampant afterwards, exacting another toll on the survivors. Even the dead were not left undisturbed. The Storm uprooted hundreds of graves and crypts, lodging many caskets in trees. Other caskets were later found washed into the Gulf.

Lack of water was the most pressing concern after the hurricane. Fortunately, the pipes that carried water from the artesian wells at Alta Loma located 18 miles from the City on the Texas mainland remained undamaged. The wrecked pumping station was repaired within a few days, after which water flowed to the City.

The editor then gave an explanation on the mechanics of hurricanes:

The cyclone could be thought of as a gigantic propeller blade. The bands of clouds produce the heavy rains and cyclonic winds. Between the bands can be diminished wind with little rain. The wind and rain waxes and wanes as these bands spin around. The closer to the eye wall of the hurricane, the stronger are the winds.

Within the eye of the storm is a low-pressure vacuum that raises the level of seawater. When this elevated area of sea reaches land, it causes a tidal surge similar to that of a tsunami.

Galveston was subject to two storm surges: The winds from the North pushed the water from the Bay onto the Island and then about 7:00 p.m. the tidal surge, created by the eye, pushed water over the Island from the Gulf side bringing with it a mountain of water 16 ft. high. The southern winds along with the surge from the Gulf side carried many victims and debris north and out into the Bay.

Even the very stars and moon seemed to conspire against the city: In the worst possible scenario, the eye passed 40 miles west of the City thus allowing the right flank, the most powerful portion of The Hurricane to directly hit the City. After traveling from the west coast of Africa, and then unimpeded after reaching Cuba, for another stretch of 800 miles, it hit Galveston at a perfect right angle. The Storm hit with a full moon overhead, and the gravitational attraction of that celestial body allowed The Storm to strike at high tide, adding to the height of the wall of water that crashed into the City.

The weeks that followed the Storm brought intense scrutiny to the Weather Bureau. *"The Galveston Daily News"* published numerous investigative articles that exposed the Weather Bureau Service bungling of the tragedy. It was pointed out that in August, mere weeks before The Hurricane, Willis Moore, the Chief of the U.S, Weather Bureau in Washington D.C., banned all cables relating to weather that were broadcast by Cuban weather observers. This proved to be a tragic mistake as demonstrated by a dispatch written by Lorenzo Gangoite, the director of the Belen Observatory in Havana, which appeared in the Cuban newspaper, *"La Lucha"*, on that very Saturday, September 8. The dispatch read that according to the type of clouds seen as well as their color and movement, Gangoite believed that the Storm that dumped more than ten inches of rain over Cuba on Monday, September 3, was now a hurricane in central Texas. The official forecast as issued by Moore, on the other hand, and received via telegraph by Isaac Cline at Galveston was that the weather system that had deluged Cuba was traveling North and was to be felt along the lower portion of the middle Atlantic coast by Friday night.

Galveston: 1900 A Storm, A Story of Twin Flames

CHAPTER 40

The Butterfly

Old Cemetery

In the distance I could now hear a car approaching, it was Alan. He pulled up to the curb of the Villa and I got in the vehicle. The roses were lying on the front passenger seat of the car.

"Take Broadway all the way West to 43rd." I said.

"To the Old City Cemetery, sir?"

"Yes."

Under cloudy but clearing skies, we drove in silence to our destination. In 1900, this was the very outskirts of the City. I exited the limo with the dozen red roses in hand. Alan would wait in the car. I proceeded into the Cemetery. The grounds were filled with countless sunflowers that swayed in the light breeze. Throughout the plot were a great variety of crypts, crosses and statues. Many of these markers were dramatic in size as well as in artistic detail. The Cemetery, like the City of 1900, reflected the exquisite artistry of the last century.

As I proceeded to the corner of the Cemetery where Genevieve rested, I could not help but notice how many markers bore the very same tragic date: September 8, 1900. I also noticed how dramatically weathered and stained with dark, unsightly streaks of soot many of the older vaults and markers were.

At the far corner, I saw the large oak tree with the twelve-foot monument underneath it. The prodigious stone marker was carved from the finest pink marble from the quarry at Marble Falls, Texas. It read:

Genevieve Petrokov

Born April 2, 1879

Died September 18, 1900

Loving Wife and Daughter- In Our Hearts She Remains Forever

Above this was a sizable pedestal upon which an angel stood. The adorable angel, emanated grace and charm. She had her head slightly tilted back, eyes gazing heavenward. Her wings were lying flat against her back in a pose of serenity mingled with a touch of contemplative sadness. I carefully arranged the red roses in the permanent vase that was affixed to the headstone.

I now closed my eyes feeling the breeze while I cleared my mind, letting her know that here I had returned on her birthday with a promise fulfilled.

I reflected that here next to her grave, my heart was so near hers. My heart feeling like an empty coffin of endless yearning, so longing for those days when we were together.

When I opened my eyes again, something remarkable caught my eye. Something marvelous and yet unexpected. There perched at the feet of the angel was a solitary Monarch butterfly, its stained glass-like, orange and black patterned wings daintily moving back and forth. A sudden whiff then stirred and carried the Monarch away. I looked around to see if there were any others, but none were to be found. As I slowly made my way out of the Cemetery, I thought what a curiosity it was to see a single, solitary Monarch butterfly, so improbable and so early in the season.

Galveston: 1900 A Storm, A Story of Twin Flames

Galveston: 1900 A Storm, A Story of Twin Flames

CHAPTER 41

Hotel Galvez

The Hotel Galvez

203

We were now riding to the Hotel Galvez, where I had made reservations for our stay. Alan had turned on the radio, which was playing the Big Band sounds that were popular at the time. During a commercial interruption, the headlines for the day were announced: *"On the European Front, the 1st and 9th Army divisions linked up to cut off more that 300,000 German troops from the 5th and 15th Panzer Divisions in the Ruhr of Germany. On the Pacific Front, US Army and Marines began the invasion of Okinawa."*

As we approached Sea Wall Boulevard located on the Gulf side of the Island, The Galvez Hotel came into view. A six story brick and concrete Spanish styled building with a red tiled roof and delicate turrets. It was built in 1911, a replacement to The Beach Hotel, and touted as fire proof. We checked in with the porters helping us to our rooms on the fifth floor.

Our rooms faced the Gulf, and I now took a look outside. The day was now partly cloudy with a steady breeze blowing from the Gulf. The water was blue green with bands of gentle whitecaps rolling onto the shore.

From this vantage, I saw how different the City looked as compared to the last time I was here. Where the Island met the sea now stood a seventeen-foot sea wall that had been built to protect the City. It had been completed by 1910. Over two thousand building that had survived The Storm had been raised using manual screw jacks. Ships that dredged sand from the Gulf pumped endless tons of sand under these structures and thus raised this portion of the Island.

Motels, restaurants, large souvenir shops, and gas stations, now occupied what was once the domain of the ramshackle structures that comprised the Midway. Looking to my right, I could see Murdoch's Bath House followed by The Breakers Bath House and then Pleasure Pier. I now rested on the bed for a short period of time before heading down stairs to the restaurant. The recall of memories had left me physically and mentally drained. As I lay on the bed in the world between partial consciousness and sleep, I thought I heard the wind howling outside.

CHAPTER 42

Dinner At the Galvez

As the elevator opened to the lobby, I walked toward the dining room located on the right side of the Hotel. Above me, I now saw a magnificent chandelier, its columnar shaped, opaque dome glass covers shining with bright light. It sparked a reminiscence of the fabulous gas chandelier that once hung in the dining room of my Villa.

The host greeted me and escorted me to the table where Alan was sitting. I sat on the chair across from Alan, facing the huge semicircular window that provided an exquisite view of the Gulf. At the horizon, I saw small groups of cumulus clouds and the light from the sun reflected brightly on these as well as the incoming surf. In front of the dining room seated at a piano was an older colored man playing. By the piano on a stand was a large sign announcing that *The Galveston Municipal Band* would be playing at the Hotel on Saturday. The pianist was playing a rendition of *"As Time Goes By"*, a song that was both beautiful and poignant. The waiter now brought us our drinks and then took our order.

"Congratulations on the news from Dr. Flemming," Alan said.

"Thank you..." My reply sounded flat.

"Some in the papers called it a complete victory over bacterial disease." He cheerfully replied.

I paused and not knowing what to say, remarked. "Just half, Alan... just half."

A strange, uncomfortable silence descended upon us as we ate our meal. After dessert, Alan told me about some of the things he read on the framed displays, photos and paintings that decorated the walls of the lobby: The Hotel had been completed in 1911 and was touted as a fireproof replacement to The Beach Hotel. Galveston Island was first discovered in the sixteenth century by a shipwrecked flotilla led by *Cabeza De Vaca*. These Spaniards named the island *"Malhado"* or isle of doom. I was stunned to think how prophetic their words would prove to be. The local Karankawa Indians befriended De Vaca before the latter left with his men on a seven-year trek to Mexico City. Later Galveston Bay would become a rendezvous point for the pirate Jean Lafitte.

The City had been named in honor of Bernardo Galvez, a Spanish military leader who served in the late 1700's as colonial Governor of Cuba and Louisiana. He aided the Thirteen Colonies in their quest for independence and actually led forces that defeated the British during the Revolutionary battle of Pensacola. After the Revolution, he was recognized by the American Congress for his efforts and even rode to the right side of George Washington during the Parade of July 4th.

I half smiled at Alan, amused at how much this young man loved history. When it came to tidbits of historical information, he had become quite a master. He then continued by informing me that *"The International Pageant of Pulchritude"* the predecessor of the Miss Universe Contest had had its origins in Galveston, Texas. The first contest was held in 1926 as an attempt to stimulate the local economy. During these contests the population on the Island often tripled. The winner of this event, which featured contestants from various countries, was awarded the title *"Miss Universe."*

"Thanks, Alan. That was quite fascinating." I said as he finished.

"My pleasure, sir."

I wiped my mouth one final time with the cloth napkin and placed it on the table.

"I'm going to change. You can fetch the vehicle while I return."

"Very well, sir."

With that I paid the bill and made my way up to my room.

CHAPTER 43

At the Beach

Galveston: 1900 A Storm, A Story of Twin Flames

Once again, Alan and I were in the limo. I had changed into a casual short sleeve shirt, shorts, and sandals. In my hands I cradled the five white roses and single red one. We were driving slowly west along Seawall Boulevard and when we approached Murdoch's Bath House, I instructed Alan to park just ahead. He found a spot on the esplanade and did so. Looking out the window, I beheld a horizon of bright yellow-orange evening light dotted with a few solitary billowing clouds.

I exited the car with the roses in hand and proceeded along the sidewalk until I located the steep concrete stairs that led down to the beach. This stairway was directly in front of *The Breakers Bath House*. To the left was *Murdoch's Bath House*. Looking right I saw *Pleasure Pier*, which I had read was the newly completed Art-Deco landmark that housed a cafe, a convention hall, and open-air stadium. At the very end of that pier, I saw a number of fishermen casting lines into the Gulf.

As I slowly proceeded down the steps, I noted that the *Bath Houses* were almost identical in appearance. They were impressive in scale, sleek white verandas with slanted red roofs capped with a central cupola. They reminded me of the Grandstands at Churchill Downs. Making my way now along the beach, the *Bath Houses* towered above me. From where I tread, I could hear the sharp, stiff flutter of their three flags, one above the cupola and another two on either end of the roof, flapping in the wind.

I veered left between *The Breakers* and *Murdoch's* and then paused. The Breakers was the very spot where *The Beach Hotel* once stood. Two city blocks beyond *The Breakers*, there in the Gulf was where *Pagoda* once stood, the very spot where Genevieve and I had our first intimate conversation. Resentment arose within as I realized how both the hand of Nature and man had altered this area, so consecrated to me. As striking as these buildings were, they were as far as I was concerned, eye sores that had usurped the irreplaceable.

Proceeding toward the surf, the salty air filled my lungs, and I stepped out of my sandals just before the water's edge. Walking into the edge of the surf, the coolness of the water momentarily stunned me. A forceful gust of wind now greeted my face. I commenced wading into water that was shin deep. The setting sun behind me was coloring the sky with shades of deep umber and burnt orange. The isolated clouds were now cast in pinkish tones highlighted by crimson and light purple.

I carefully released the five white roses into the surf: One each for Peter, Karina, Sasha, Sergei and Annie. I never saw nor came to know what happened to any of them. My eyes filled with tears as I watched the five roses carried out by the tide.

Now I took the red rose and kissed it before releasing it into the water in front of me. As it drifted into the far distance, becoming only a red speck floating on distant waves, I had a fleeting urge to follow it all the way to the very bowels of the Gulf, a journey of forward motion from which I would not return. I closed my eyes, the wind softly humming in my ears.

As I opened my eyes, I was struck by some shift in the sky. Somehow I knew, I could feel, that there was something different about it. I first noted the coloration. For a brief moment, I considered that perhaps its colors were more vivid or ... intense. No, that wasn't it. I could see that the casts had remained the same. Then I felt a sensation, unexplainable, that began to arise from within me, ascending like rekindled embers that had died so long ago... Embers of tranquility and reassurance.

I again scanned the sky, and then I saw it. To my left, I detected a single, unique cloud, high above drifting slowly my way. But it was something in the very shape of the cloud that really caught my attention. Something discernible. My mouth dropped. I blinked my eyes to make sure I was not seeing things...

Yes, there was no doubt. I studied the shape closely. The cloud, although nebulous at its edges, had the unmistakable form of the heart locket that Genevieve so treasured.

Like a strobe of lighting, an epiphany of consciousness and absolution then hit me, suddenly and all at once. Waves of self-forgiveness overtook my being. Waves that seemed to be magnified by the repercussions of the surf that lapped at my legs, and the puffs of wind that blew at my face. In her own magnanimous way, and one in which only she could show me, Genevieve was revealing to me the true meaning of Love. She also was showing me that I was not, nor had I ever been alone. Through this cloud she was giving me a sign and a message. A message of timelessness and eternal truth. A still small voice that I heard now as a gentle, serene whisper in my ears, filling me with reassurance. A message about the meaning of genuine and absolute Love... Love at its most essential core.

Through her, I fathomed, at that moment, that Love is the very bond, the crucial element, which the Architect of Creation uses to envelop all the cosmos together. It was and is the very inspiration for the genesis of the Cosmos.

The words, purifying and welcoming, flowed to me:

> *The Almighty's desire to give and share his Love is the very reason that the cosmic Vessel, which we call the Universe, was formed. And we, created in the image of the Divine can suffuse a being, a vessel, fashioned not only of flesh and blood, but also of Soul, with Love. By us summoning, with our very own volition, the better angels of our nature, and choosing this kind of Love in its most pure, true essence, we unite with the One of all eternities.*

The completion of the thought then dawned upon me: When we bring to fruition these words, we fulfill the process begun by the Almighty, and complete the circle of creation, an endless, unified, cosmic flow of time, space and energy.

I am eternally grateful... forever.. For Genevieve, my Princess, and her illumination and how her life with me and her Love, filled with absolute adoration, unveiled this cardinal insight to me.

Although I was standing fully cognizant of the cool water bathing my legs and the grainy sand beneath the soles of my feet, at that very moment I was even more mindful that there is a dimension much more consequential to this world than just the level of physical sensation, a level beyond space and beyond even time. I know that although Genevieve and I appeared to be apart, we are really at One. At the most supernal level, we have always been together. A Twin Flame that can never, ever be consumed.

She showed me that there is bliss, a Heaven here on Earth, and that it is obtainable by complete, absolute, unconditional, wholehearted Amour. Her life, as magnificent and fleeting as a passing rainbow, still has a permanence that no Storm, no Thing, could ever erase or destroy.

That permanence is the endless, unbounded, eternal Love we share, and that very energy, like nourishing rays of sunlight, permeated every grain of sand on the beach where I was standing. It will permeate every step I take no matter where that may be, till the end of my days.... I stood there for what seemed a long time, bathed in the perfection of the moment, feeling the Gulf breeze, the purifying water on my legs.... feeling the shackles fall off my soul.

Galveston: 1900 A Storm, A Story of Twin Flames

Somewhere, high above, an angel smiled.

"When love is lost, do not bow your head in sadness;
instead keep your head up high and gaze into
heaven for that is where your broken
heart has been sent to heal."
- Unknown

"In the depth of winter, I finally learned that there was within me an invincible summer."

-Albert Camus

Galveston: 1900 A Storm, A Story of Twin Flames

Galveston: 1900 A Storm, A Story of Twin Flames

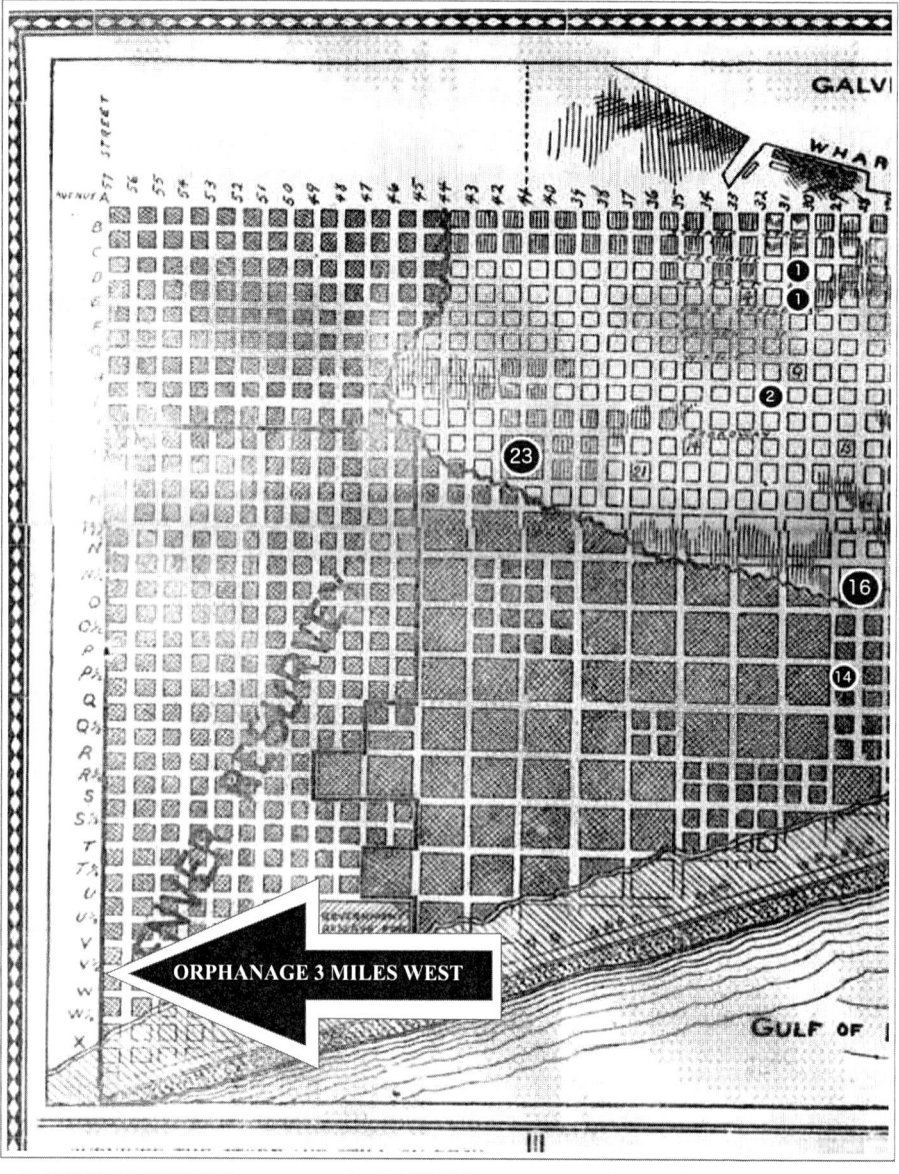

1- COTTON PRESSES	7- MASONIC TEMPLE	13- DR. YOUNG'S HOUSE
2- PLANTER COMPRESSES	8- URI'S VILLA	14- GENEVIEVE'S HOUSE
3- TEXAS STAR FLOUR MILLS	9- TEMPLE B'INAI ISRAEL	15- ROSENBURG'S WOMEN'S HOME
4- GALVESTON SHOE & HAT CO.	10- HOTEL GALVEZ	16- GARTEN VEREIN
5- LEVY BUILDING	11- MURDOCH'S	17- ROSENBURG SCHOOL
6- HARMONY HALL	12- ISAAC'S HOUSE	18- THE TREMONT HOTEL

Galveston: 1900 A Storm, A Story of Twin Flames

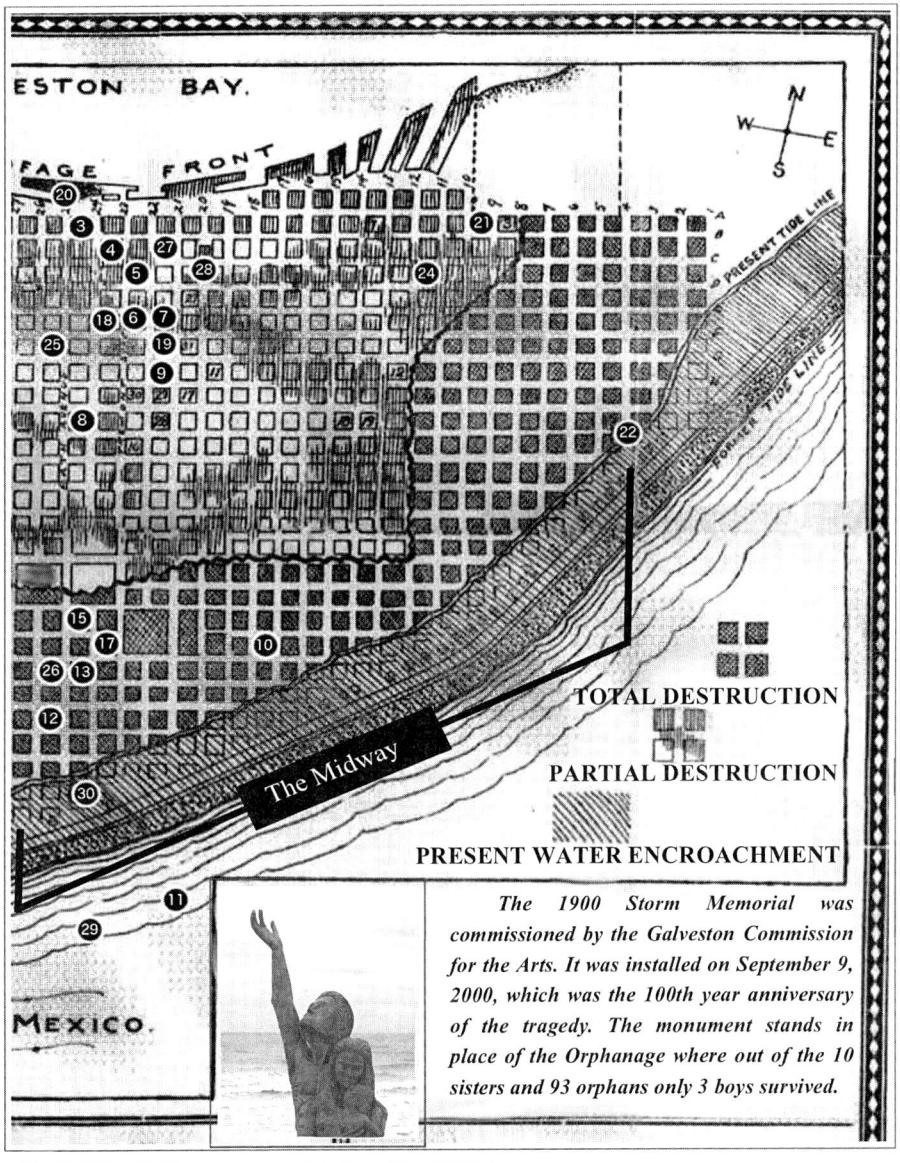

The 1900 Storm Memorial was commissioned by the Galveston Commission for the Arts. It was installed on September 9, 2000, which was the 100th year anniversary of the tragedy. The monument stands in place of the Orphanage where out of the 10 sisters and 93 orphans only 3 boys survived.

19- BALL HIGH SCHOOL
20- UNION RAILROAD
21- OLD RED
22- LUCAS TERRACE
23- CEMETERY
24- LOUISE HOPKIN'S BOARDING HOME
25- GRAND OPERA
26- BATH AVE PUBLIC SCHOOL
27- GALVESTON PRINTING CO.
28- CITY HALL
29- PAGODA BATH HOUSE
30- THE BEACH HOTEL

MAP OF GALVESTON:
Courtesy of the Rosenberg Library, Galveston, Texas

About The Author

Ervin Mendlovitz. OD lives in San Antonio, Texas where he has a private optometric practice. He has a passion for writing, taking care of his patients, and studying mystic wisdom. He is married to his wife Elizabeth, and they have two sons, Aaron and Bryan.

Dr. Mendlovitz developed a love for Galveston ever since first visiting the city as a child for the first time in the early 1970's when he became fascinated by the historic buildings of the city and the story of The Storm.

To learn more about Ervin Mendlovitz, O.D. and his practice visit us at: http://on.fb.me/1iHFCda

For Galveston historical photographs & vintage film by Thomas A. Edison showing The Storm's aftermath
visit: http://on.fb.me/1n1BWKj